BUGSY

BY WAY OF EXPLANATION

The story of Bugsy Malone takes place in New York, in 1929. It's a world of would-be gangsters, show-girls and dreamers. But it's a world where you never see an adult. And, as they say in the movies, all the parts are played by kids.

If you're a young reader, you won't have any trouble imagining yourself in the story. If you're a little older . . . well, you'll just have to imagine a little harder.

Alan Parker was born in Islington, London, in 1944. Giving up all hopes of being a brain surgeon and nuclear scientist, he started work as a post boy for an advertising agency and was mistaken for a copywriter for a number of years. In 1970 he set up his own film commercial company, and has since directed hundreds of commercials, winning so many awards around the world that his mother's mantelpiece collapsed. In 1975 he won a television 'Emmy' award for directing the B.B.C. film *'The Evacuees'*. He went on to write and direct *'Bugsy Malone'*, his first feature film as well as his first book.

Married, he lives in London with his four children, to whom this book is dedicated and who claim to have written most of it.

Bugsy Malone

by ALAN PARKER

AN ARMADA ORIGINAL

Bugsy Malone was first published in 1976 in Armada by
Wm. Collins Sons & Co. Ltd., 14 St. James's Place,
London SW1A 1PF
Reprinted 1976

Printed in Great Britain by
Wm. Collins Sons & Co. Ltd., Glasgow

CONTENTS

For Lucy, Alexander, Jake and Nathan,
who heard it first

1. ROXY

Someone once said that if it was raining brains, Roxy Robinson wouldn't even get wet. In all of New York they didn't come much dumber than Roxy the Weasel. In short, Roxy was a dope—and he fulfilled people's expectations of him by taking the blind alley down the side of Henry's Smokes Store, on the corner of Orchard and Hester.

Overhead, the rusty, broken gutter turned the rainwater into a nasty brown liquid that gushed out on to the sidewalk below. It had been raining all night, and a sizeable pool had formed. Roxy's frantic feet disturbed the neon reflections. He felt the icy water seep through his spats and bite into his ankles. He'd been running for a dozen blocks, and although his legs felt strong, his lungs were giving out on him.

He skidded to a halt as he noticed the wall at the end of the blind alley. Anyone else would have seen it a hundred yards back, but not Roxy. Whatever passed for a brain between his ears whirled into action as he considered his options. He ducked into a doorway. At the end of the alley, the red neon light glowed and dimmed in time with Roxy's heartbeats, and the big reflected letters of 'Henry's Smokes Store' spread across the wet road. Roxy's heartbeats moved into second gear as four black shadows appeared and gobbled up the red neon.

Roxy had spent his whole life making two and two into five, but he could smell trouble like other people can smell gas. The four shadows became sharper as they gave way to four neatly pressed suits. They looked as snazzy as a Fifth Avenue store window—only these guys were no dummies.

Roxy collided with a trash can as he started running again. It clattered loudly on to the sidewalk, disturbing the slumber of a ginger cat, which scooted across his path. Roxy reached the wall in seconds, desperately clawing at the bricks to get a handhold at the top. But it was too high

7

and Roxy was no jumper. He turned to face his pursuers.

They advanced together, their violin cases dangling at their sides, like a sinister chorus line. Ten yards from him they stopped. The cases opened. Click. Click. Click. Click. Roxy blinked, in unison, and a bead of sweat found its way out from under his hat brim and dribbled down his forehead. From their cases, the hoods took out four immaculate, shiny, new guns. Roxy stared at them in disbelief.

Suddenly, one of them spoke.

'Your name Robinson?'

Roxy nodded. His own name was one of the few things he had learned in school.

'Roxy Robinson?' The hood's voice spat out once more. 'You work for Fat Sam?'

Roxy's adam's apple bobbed around frantically in his throat as if it was trying to find a way out. He managed to force his neck muscles to shake his head into a passable nod.

It was all the hoods needed. Almost immediately, the wall was peppered with what can only be described as custard pies. Roxy briefly eyed the sight, not quite believing his good fortune. His optimism was short-lived as a large quantity of slimy, foamy liquid enveloped his sharp, weasel-like features. His ears protruded like toby jug handles from the creamy mess.

The hoods clicked their violin cases shut, turned, and with a confident strut walked back up the alley. The splurge gun had claimed its first victim—and whatever game it was that everyone was playing, sure as eggs is eggs, Roxy Robinson was out of it.

2. BLOUSEY

Blousey Brown had always wanted to be famous. She got the bug very early—at the age of three she gave an impromptu recital for her family at Thanksgiving. She would tap dance a little and sing some, and what her rather squeaky voice lacked in volume she made up for with enthusiasm. Her audience was always especially encouraging. But what family doesn't have a talented child? In fact, there had been vaudeville acts in Blousey's family since way back. They hadn't gathered a great deal of fame amongst them—the yellowed notices in the cuttings book weren't too plentiful—but they were remembered with great affection. At Thanksgiving, when Blousey put on her shiny red tap shoes with the pink bows and did her annual turn, someone would say, 'She's got it all right. You can tell she's gonna be famous. There's a kind of sparkle in her eye. Bravo, Blousey. Bravo.'

It was the last 'Bravo' that did it. Since that moment, Blousey had been hooked on show business.

Life wasn't easy—sometimes she wondered if it was all worth it. Like now.

She clicked open her compact and quickly repaired her make-up. She fixed her lipstick and pinched the wave in her hair. One dollar eighty that wave had cost and already it was straightening out. The guy in the beauty parlour had said she looked terrific, and she hadn't been about to argue. What girl didn't like looking pretty? She had parted with her dollar eighty gladly. She checked the crumpled piece of paper in her hand once more. Scribbled in pencil were the words: *Fat Sam's Grand Slam Speakeasy. Audition 10 o'clock.*

The note had been given to her by a friend who had been in the chorus at Sam's and had got Blousey the audition. The friend hadn't written down the address, of course. Speakeasies were against the law and the Grand Slam's location behind Pop Becker's bookstore was a secret. As it happens, it was probably the worst kept secret in town, because half of New York went to Sam's place for their late night entertainment.

Blousey had pushed her way across the floor of the crowded, smoky speakeasy, following her friend's instructions: up the stairs to the backstage corridor that led to the girls' changing room and the boss's office. A screen of frosted glass with neat geometric shapes etched on the panes formed the wall between the office and the corridor. On the door, printed in rather aggressive gold letters, was '*S. Stacetto. Private.*'

Blousey sat on a wicker-back bentwood double seater,

to which she had been shown by a nasty-looking character who had cracked his knuckles as he said, 'Sit there, lady. The boss will sees yuh in a minute.' Some minute. The minute had stretched itself to an hour and a half and she was still waiting.

Blousey ferreted nervously in her battered leather bag. She had brought too many clothes with her as usual, but she reassured herself that one never knew which number they'd ask for. Her bag was also extra heavy because of her books and baseball bat. The books were very precious to Blousey. They were old, with stiff-backed covers, and Blousey had read them and re-read them till she knew every page. Ever since she had been out of work she'd feared she might come back to her apartment one day to find that her landlady had taken them by way of rent. So she took no chances. Where she went, they went. The baseball bat was for protection. From what, she was never sure. She wasn't even sure if she could lift it—let alone swing it—but, like the books, it went with her everywhere.

All around her in the corridor, the chorus girls trotted back and forth in their stage outfits, a flurry of sequins, organza, and orange feathers. Blousey blushed a little at the sly and giggly glances they threw in her direction. She breathed a heavy sigh. She had decided to sit it out, no matter what. Fat Sam's black janitor whistled a bluesy melody as he swept up around her. Blousey politely lifted her feet for him to sweep under. She was beginning to feel fed up and just a little tired. She rested her head against the wall and listened to the speakeasy band as the lively music found its way backstage.

Suddenly, the music was mixed with the muffled sound of agitated voices coming from Fat Sam's office, behind the frosted glass partition.

3. FAT SAM

Fat Sam's podgy hand wrestled with the selector knob on the shiny mahogany, fretwork-fronted radio. As he found the right station, the high-pitched frequency whistle gave way to the drone of a news announcer, who blurted out his message.

'We interrupt this programme of music to bring you an important news flash . . . Reports are coming in of a gangland incident on the Lower East Side, involving a certain Robert Robinson, known to the police as "Roxy the Weasel", and believed to be a member of the gang of alleged mobster king, Fat Sam Stacetto. Robinson was the victim of a sensational attack, and we go over to our reporter on the spot for a . . .'

Before the news announcer could finish, Fat Sam snatched at the on/off knob on the radio. Fat Sam was not pleased. Like most hoodlums, he had clawed his way up from the streets to get a little recognition. A little notoriety. But whenever he ever made the papers or the newscasts it made him mad. Very mad.

'Alleged mobster king of the Lower East Side,' was it? There was no 'alleged' about it. Sam was king of these parts. There wasn't a racket or a shady deal in which he didn't have his fat podgy finger. No, there was no doubt. At least, not in Fat Sam's mind. But he was to find out that others thought differently before the night was out.

He paced up and down on the red turkey carpet that fronted the desk in his office. The rest of his gang stood around in silence. They had learned from bitter experience not to talk at times like these.

Fat Sam stopped pacing, and snatched a wooden pool cue from the rack. He stepped forward to the pool table. One of his men moved forward with the box. No one ever mentioned the box, but unless Fat Sam stood on it there was no way he could possibly reach the pool table. Sam stabbed at the first ball. To everyone's relief it thudded down into the corner pocket. With the box preceding him, Fat Sam stalked around the table and, as he potted the balls one by one, he shouted, 'So tell me how you allow this to happen? Roxy was one of my best. What have you got to say for yourselves, you bunch of dummies? Knuckles? Louis? Ritzy? Angelo? Snake-Eyes?' Fat Sam's gang looked at each other uneasily. They always agreed with everything Fat Sam said. They weren't stupid.

Sitting by the water cooler was Knuckles, Fat Sam's number one man. He cracked his knuckles often, which is how he got his name. It always looked a little threatening as he idly clicked at the bones in his hands, but to tell the truth it was more nerves than bravado—though Knuckles never let on. He had a name to live up to and he was determined to do it.

Louis was called Louis because he resembled Shakedown Louis, a hero in these parts. No one ever knew Shakedown Louis, or what he did, but he had a name and it was enough for anyone that Louis resembled him. And anyway, whoever heard of a hoodlum called Joshuah Spleendecker. Mrs Spleendecker preferred Louis. And most of all Louis preferred Louis.

Snake-Eyes got his name because of those two little ivory cubes that clicked and clicked away in his palm. He had been the king of any street corner crap game ever since he learned that a dice has six faces and a hood only needs two.

Ritzy was the quietest of the bunch. He was a dapper dresser, with knife-edged creases down his trousers that could cut your throat. Ritzy was one of those people who always look like they've come straight from the laundry. He had starched eyelids, ears neatly pressed and steamed, and even his smile seemed to crease his face like it had been freshly applied by the best laundry in Chinatown.

Angelo was called Angelo because his mother thought it was a cute name. It was also his father's name, and his grandfather's name, which meant that the chances of his being called Clarence or Albin were pretty slim.

'Call yourselves hoodlums?' Fat Sam was saying.

'You're a disgrace to your profession, do you hear me? A disgrace. And most of all you're a disgrace to Fat Sam.'

Fat Sam poked his chest proudly with his thumb. He mopped at his forehead with his handkerchief. Still the gang remained motionless. Fat Sam walked to the drinks cupboard. He yanked at the handle and pulled down the veneered front flap. He took out a crystal decanter of orange juice, and toyed with it as he spoke.

'We all know who's behind this, don't we?'

The gang replied in mechanical unison. 'Sure do, Boss.'

'You don't need a head full of brains to know that, do you?'

'Sure don't, Boss.'

'We all know who's been monkeying us around, don't we?'

'Oh yeah, Boss. We sure know.'

'So who it is, you dummies? Tell me who?'

The gang looked at one another for a moment. They weren't sure if they should risk mentioning that dreaded name in Fat Sam's office. They decided together. They were all wrong.

'Dandy Dan, Boss.'

Fat Sam was so incensed he fell off his box. His face bloated out to become a passable imitation of a Christmas balloon. He screamed, 'Don't mention that man's name in this office.'

The gang redeemed themselves by picking him up and brushing him down. Fat Sam seethed away and steam seemed to squirt from his ears. Suddenly there was a knock at the door, and the gang stiffened visibly. Ritzy looked even starchier, Snake-Eyes clicked at his dice, Knuckles cracked his knuckles. Louis pulled back his shoulders, shot out his cuffs and did his impersonation of Shakedown Louis. Fat Sam kept his dignity. After all, he was Fat Sam.

'Come in,' he said.

The door opened, and a curly blonde head popped nervously around it. It was Blousey. She had finally tired of waiting and had plucked up the courage to come in. The gang looked at her incredulously.

'Er . . . Mr Stacetto, I'm Miss Blousey Brown. I've come about the job. I'm a dancer.'

Fat Sam couldn't believe his ears. He bellowed. 'A

dancer! A dancer! Believe me, honey, right now I don't need a dancer. Come back tomorrow.'

Blousey retreated in despair, but before she could close the door, the little janitor, who had been waiting behind her for his chance, also made his plea for showbiz stardom.

'Er . . . Mr Stacetto, I wondered if I could have my audition . . . Last week you said . . .'

Before he could finish, Fat Sam had jumped in feet first and trampled on his sentence. 'Am I going mad? Fizzy, will you get out of here.'

Fizzy had anticipated the answer. It wasn't new to him, and he ducked out of the room as Sam's words hit the door. In his speedy exit, he forgot that he'd left his bucket outside and put his foot in it, toppling headlong over Blousey as he retreated.

Inside, Fat Sam continued to bellow at his gang.

'Dancers! Dancers! I'm surrounded by mamby—pamby dancers, singers, piano players, banjo players, tin-whistle players—at a time when I need brains, you hear me, *brains*. Brains and muscles.'

The last words sizzled the gang's eardrums and rattled the pictures on the wall. Knuckles took it upon himself to speak for the rest. He offered meekly, 'You've got us, Boss!'

Knuckles took the soda siphon from the shelf and attempted to top up Fat Sam's glass of orange juice. The soda water went many places but Fat Sam's glass wasn't one of them. Sam looked down at his drenched suit.

'You! You great hunk of lard. Your trouble is you've got muscle where you ought to have brains. My canary's got more brains than you, you dumb salami!'

Fat Sam pulled Knuckles' hat over his head, snatched the siphon and squirted it at him. As the soda water dripped from his face, Ritzy, Louis, and Snake-Eyes giggled nervously. That was a mistake.

Sam turned to them, siphon poised. 'So what's funny? Something make you laugh?'

The remainder of the gang felt the full force of the soda as it bounced from hood to hood, leaving their sharp, smiling faces damp and droopy.

Outside in the corridor, Fizzy the janitor helped

14

Blousey with her things. She picked up her heavy case and straightened her hat. Fizzy offered her a little consolation.

'Don't worry, honey, I've been trying to see him for months and months.'

'You have? What do you do?'

'I'm only the greatest tap dancer on earth.'

'You are?'

'Of course I are. Cross my heart.' Fizzy's heart must have been in a funny place because he crossed his face. 'But all he ever says is come back tomorrow. I ask you, how many times can I come back tomorrow?'

Blousey smiled. For a moment she looked like she couldn't care less about the cancelled interview. But she was pretending.

4. BUGSY (AT LAST)

Out in the street, the sidewalk still glistened from the rain. The sign in the lighted window said *'Pop Becker's Book Emporium. Books, Books and more Books. From 5 cents.'* And another read *'A book is cheaper than a steak. Read one, learn a little, and maybe you'll eat better.'* The window of Pop's store was crammed with books of every description.

Bugsy Malone looked at his reflection in the glass. He straightened his tie and tilted his hat to a smart, acceptable angle. He pulled at the bottom of his jacket and, for a moment, the creases vanished—but promptly sprang back again. Bugsy wasn't the smartest guy in town, but he had an air about him that was difficult to describe. A sort of inner dignity that didn't rely on crisp white cuffs and a diamond stick pin. He was no hood. He'd been around them, sure. He'd had his scrapes. And he generally came out on top. But he got a funny kind of pleasure just from being in the middle of things. Always there, but never involved. He'd been quite a useful boxer in his day, too. Except for one slight handicap. He had a jaw that had more glass in it than Macy's front window. But he still kept in trim. Made a few bucks—from 'this and that', he liked to say. In the main they were honest bucks—looking for promising fighters and steering them in the direction of Cagey Joe at Sluggers Gym. Cagey Joe would teach them all he knew. And he knew a lot. If they made out, Bugsy made a few bucks. To date, he hadn't found a Jack Johnson, but he'd made enough to pay his rent and treat himself to the occasional turkey dinner. And this was at a time when a bowl of soup and a crust of bread was Sunday lunch for most people.

Bugsy pushed open the door of the bookstore. A brass bell rang. Behind the counter, Pop Becker looked up from his dinner. He peered at Bugsy over the top of his glasses and underneath his green eye shield.

'Hi, Bugsy.'

'Hi, Pop.'

Without another word, Pop swivelled in his chair and passed over a small, red, leather-bound book. It wasn't asked for but it was received without question.

'Thanks, Pop.'

Pop waved, not looking up from his racing paper or his dinner of salt beef and pickled cucumber, which he munched with as little enthusiasm as he had shown to his customer. Bugsy opened the book and placed a dollar bill inside. He moved to the side of the store. The whole wall was a mass of heavy books on creaking shelves. He tapped on one of them and a row of six books disappeared to reveal a small peep-hole. The tubby face of Jelly filled the hole.

'Hi, Bugsy.'

'Hi, Jelly.'

Bugsy passed the book to Jelly, who took out the dollar bill. He reached down and pulled back the whole wall of books, which moved as one. Revealed was the smoky, noisy hubbub of Fat Sam's speakeasy.

Bugsy walked through and stood for a moment at the top of the stairs that led down to the speakeasy floor. Jelly pulled the door closed behind him. On stage, the Fat Sam Grand Slam Speakeasy show had begun. Razamataz, the leader of the band, pounded away at his piano, belting out the music that couldn't be found anywhere else in town. At least, that's what Fat Sam used to say. And, for the most part, his regular customers would agree with him.

Centre stage was Tallulah. She was the star of the show and everyone knew it. Her hair was a work of art, patiently created at Madame Monzani's Hair Parlour. She peeped out from behind her curls with eyes that were wide open—but could narrow to a cool stare that cut guys in half. And often did. Tallulah was as cool as they come, and she pouted her red cupid-bow lips as she sang her songs in that ever-so-slinky way that drew besotted stares from the guys and envious looks from the girls. She was also Sam's girl, which made life a little easier for her and a little tougher for the rest of the girls. Not that Tallulah was without talent herself. She put over a number like no one else.

Backing her were Loretta and Bangles. They dutifully filled in the musical scraps that Tallulah threw them. The other girls took care of the dancing. They were the slickest line-up in town, and their clicking, tap dancing feet would rattle away on that wooden stage with such speed and agility that they never failed to bring a gasp from the speakeasy first timers.

Bugsy walked down the stairs. He looked a little out of place in the crowd, his clothes not quite up to the standard of the other, snazzier-dressed customers. But Bugsy had a confident air that made up for his wardrobe. He stopped to talk briefly to the hat-check girl. She seemed pleased to see him and he returned her smile by kissing his finger and touching her on the nose. She liked that.

All around him, waiters and waitresses weaved their way in and out of the tables. The customers chatted amongst themselves or sat sipping their drinks, riveted by the spectacular floor show. Bugsy made his way over to the bar and leaned against the wooden counter. The sour-faced barman ignored him. He wiped and polished the glass in his hand until it sparkled. Bugsy waved to get his attention. 'Excuse me. Er . . . excuse, me, fellah.'

The barman walked up to him slowly. He scowled at Bugsy all the way.

'A double. On the rocks,' Bugsy said.

The barman took the glass he had been polishing and

17

placed it on the bar-top. He filled it with a scoop of ice and then topped it up with Coke. He didn't take his eyes off Bugsy, who tried to soften the scowl with a joke.

'You look like you put your face on backwards this morning.'

The barman fingered the lapels on Bugsy's crumpled jacket. 'I don't think much of your suit,' he said at last.

'I'll tell my tailor,' Bugsy answered.

'You've got too much mouth.'

'So I'll tell my dentist.'

Bugsy felt he had got a points decision on the encounter and moved away into the crowd. As he did so, he collided with Blousey, who was on her way to the exit. Her heavy bag crunched into his shins and the drink he was holding spilled down his suit. Bugsy let out a yell. 'Ouch! Look where you're going, will you, lady.'

'I'm sorry. I'm truly sorry.' Blousey apologised.

Bugsy brushed at his jacket and rubbed his sore shins.

'What have you got in there—an ice-hockey stick?'

'No, a baseball bat.'

'You're a baseball player. Right?'

Blousey propped herself on a stool whilst she straightened herself out. 'No. I'm a dancer. My mother made me pack it.'

'You're a sports nut. Right?'

Blousey started moving through the crowd. Bugsy followed her. 'It's for protection, in case I get robbed,' she said.

'And you take it everywhere with you. Right?'

Blousey manoeuvred herself through the crowd. She stopped for a moment, her path blocked by a waiter who was trying to unload a precarious-looking tray of drinks. Blousey was not really in the mood to talk to Bugsy and explained reluctantly, 'I'm here about a job.'

The way she said it you would never have believed her disappointment. She wasn't about to let on to this guy, whom she didn't know from Adam, that she'd not even got past Fat Sam's office door.

Bugsy persevered. 'Did you get it?'

'They said come back tomorrow.'

She tried to lose him by taking a different direction through the crowd but Bugsy caught up with her. He made one more attempt at being friendly. 'What's your name, anyway?'

'Brown.' Blousey replied.

'Sounds like a loaf of bread.' Bugsy joked.

'Blousey Brown.'

'Sounds like a stale loaf of bread.'

Blousey's smile was one of those big phoney types that disappear the moment they are formed. Bugsy laughed at his own joke, and was about to follow it up with something a little more polite, when suddenly the music in the speakeasy was interrupted by a loud scream.

Suddenly there was pandemonium. People scrambled over themselves in an effort to get under the tables. Chairs and glasses toppled over. At the top of the stairs, four sinister-looking hoods stood in line. In their hands each one carried a splurge gun.

The hood on the left made a small, almost unnoticeable nod. It was all the signal they needed. Suddenly, with a strange slurping sound, the guns burst into life. Along the mirrored barback splattered a great white line of splurge. The barman ducked down out of sight. Fat Sam, alarmed at the sudden outburst of screaming, crashed out of his office. As he appeared at the top of his stairs, the hoods trained their guns on him. He dived for the floor. Knuckles, always a little slow, caught a splurge salvo on the arm. Then, having made their point, the hoods vanished as quickly as they had appeared, brushing Pop Becker out of the way as they did so.

Under their table, Bugsy and Blousey struggled to get out her baseball bat. They both clung to it—not really sure what to do with it. Fat Sam regained his posture and started to straighten up the overturned chairs. Nervously, he tried to reassure his customers. He fooled nobody. 'O.K., everybody, it's O.K. Nothing to worry about now. Back to your tables. The fun's over. No one can say Fat Sam's ain't the liveliest joint in town. Razamataz! Music! I wanna see everybody enjoying themselves.'

Razamataz hesitantly began playing his piano. The rest of the band joined in. The sound was a little ragged at first, but gradually it got back to normal as everybody once more began to talk, and returned to their places at the tables. Fat Sam moved to the bar. The rest of his gang, more than a little confused, followed him. Knuckles propped himself up at the bar and Sam examined his splurged arm. He touched the gooey mess of splurge and quietly looked at the end of his fingers. He looked very thoughtful, if not a little worried. He spoke softly to himself. He wouldn't have liked anyone else to know his concern.

'Dis means trouble,' he said.

5. THE SPLURGE THICKENS

On East 6th Street, by Henry's Smokes Store, the broken gutter still turned the rainwater into a nasty brown liquid that dripped on to the sidewalk. The rain had held off for a while and the pool of water had resumed its earlier puddle proportions. The bricks glistened as they caught the light from the neon signs. The ginger alley cat that had made its home in the trash cans spat as he looked upwards to the black metal fire escape. This was his alley and he hated intruders. Up there, hidden away from the flashing neon light, was a dark figure who moved slowly and secretively from shadow to shadow. The ginger cat scurried for cover, his courage deserting him, as the dark feet began to move down the iron stairs. At the bottom of the fire escape the figure stopped, and remained silent.

Shoulders had always been a little more secretive than was necessary. He liked being shady, it made him feel important. Around the corner of the alleyway a car approached. Shoulders jumped back against the wall as its lights lit up the wet street. The alley cat dashed for cover once more and took refuge in a pile of garbage. It was obvious to him that he wasn't going to get any sleep that night. A white sedan pulled to a halt. Shoulders moved out of the shadows and walked up to it. It was driven by a grey-uniformed chauffeur who never looked anywhere but ahead. He was well trained. The windows in the rear of the sedan were covered by blinds. Shoulders moved closer to one of the back windows. The white, fringed blind snapped upwards.

Inside the car sat a figure that was smart, dapper—in fact, entirely immaculate. He was dressed in an astrakhan-collared coat and carried a black cane with a silver top. His hat would have won prizes at a hatter's convention. He ran his gloved finger along his moustache which was, not surprisingly, also immaculate. There was no doubt that this man was special. There was no doubt this man had arrived on the scene. There was no doubt that, to Fat Sam, this man spelled trouble. He was Dandy Dan.

Out of the window he passed a brown leather case with reinforced corners and brass hinges.

'You know what to do?'

'Sure, Dandy Dan,' Shoulders confirmed.

Dan turned away and tapped the chauffeur on the shoulder with his cane. 'Step on it, Jackson.'

This Jackson dutifully did, and the sedan drove off into the night.

Inside the barber shop, the barber snipped away at the back of his customer's head. Not a lot of hair was cut off, but a great deal of snipping certainly gave the impression that the client was getting his money's worth. It was an old barber's trick. The head of hair belonged to Frank Bloomey, Fat Sam's lawyer. 'Flash Frankie' always called here for a haircut on his way uptown. He had a swanky office overlooking Central Park but most of his clients had premises overlooking the East River. On the wall above his desk was a framed certificate from the New York Justice Department, but everyone knew it was the downtown hoodlums who kept him in business. Flash Frankie's silver tongue could get a guy out of jail quicker than a truckload of dynamite.

He relaxed into a reclining position as the barber placed a hot towel over his face. On top of the hot towel cabinet, an old radio buzzed out a tune.

In the street outside, Shoulders crept towards the barber shop window. Shoulders always crept. He couldn't walk like ordinary people, it wouldn't have been secretive enough. Even when he went shopping he would creep from store to store. He stopped, and bent down to open

21

the case that Dandy Dan had given him. He clicked open the brass hinges and lifted the lid. Inside, laid out in neat order, were the shiny metallic components of what looked like a gun. Shoulders clicked the pieces together and the gun took shape. He loaded it up with a number of round white pellets that dropped neatly into the chamber. Then he moved towards the door of the barber's shop.

It is fair to say that Bloomey was more than a little surprised as his chair was swivelled around and the steaming hot towel pulled from his face. His eyes, like his mouth, were wide open with astonishment—in the brief moment, that is, before his face was submerged in a curious sticky mess. The splurge gun had struck again.

The violinist in Mama Lugini's Italian restaurant scratched away at the violin which was securely tucked under his chin. In fact, even when he wasn't playing and the violin was locked away in its case, his chin would clamp on an invisible instrument. Such was the effect of playing all night, every night, that his chin was permanently tucked into his shoulder. This made playing the violin very easy but sipping soup very difficult. He had practised hard at his instrument for more years than he could remember, and never forgave himself that he wasn't playing on a concert hall platform instead of to the unappreciative ears of the diners at Mama Lugini's.

A very slim gentleman sat sucking enormous quantities of spaghetti through his rather comic toothbrush moustache. His wife picked at her dinner. She never seemed to eat any—she just toyed and twirled her fork in the pasta. Her face was long and bored, which would normally have been the first thing you'd have noticed about her but for the ridiculous feathered hat she was wearing. The couple rarely spoke to one another except for the occasional, 'Irving, would you please pass the salt,' or sometimes, 'Irving, would you please pass the pepper.' This was the sum of their conversation. Irving would often make loud slurping sounds with his spaghetti, but very rarely did he speak. The violinist had little effect on either of them. He could scratch away at his Italian love songs until the strings of his violin wore through and

22

snapped—it still wouldn't have helped the conversation between Irving and his wife.

But tonight the violinist was interrupted. Not by a clumsy waiter bumping into him or by a persistent customer asking for 'O Sole Mio' for the twenty-third time. He was interrupted by something far more important. In fact, the entire front window, on which was neatly painted 'Mama Lugini's Italian Restaurant', shattered into a million pieces.

The customers looked up from their dinners and the violinist almost, but not quite, stopped playing. He looked up from his violin and saw, standing in line on the sidewalk, Dandy Dan's gang—their splurge guns gleaming in the lamplight. Irving stopped slurping.

A passing waiter was the first to move. He panicked—and dropped an enormous plate of tacky spaghetti into the coloured feathers of Irving's wife's hat. Irving himself was less fortunate, because it was he whom Dan's gang had come for. His puzzled stare demanded an answer. He got it. The splurge guns burst into action. Each one belched out its foamy white contents. Irving received the full blast head on, and immediately dropped into his spaghetti under the weight of the sticky onslaught. His wife, a bedraggled mess of spaghetti strands and loose feathers, started screaming. Her face wobbled up and down. In fact, the scream was some time coming, as her face seemed to tremble for an eternity before a piercing shriek escaped from her larynx. The other diners in the restaurant all ran for cover—so did the violinist. In fairness to him, it is true to say he kept on faithfully playing whilst he made his exit—ducking down behind the cheese counter.

The hoods, their work successfully completed, made their getaway. However, one of their number wasn't quite up to the slick behaviour of the rest of the gang, as they began to climb back into the sedan outside. It was Doodle.

Doodle had never been the cleverest of hoods and was a little out of place in the immaculate company of the Dandy Dan gang. In fact, he was almost dumb enough for Fat Sam's gang. He slipped in the doorway, and the precious splurge gun he was carrying fell to the floor and slid across the tiles. The terrified diners stared in amazement. Doodle watched their inquisitive eyes move towards the secret gun lying on the floor. The gun he had been told to guard with his life. He was unsure what to do. He floundered in the restaurant while his worried little piggy eyes darted about behind his spectacles. One of the other hoods came back in to pull him out.

'Doodle, get out of here.'

'But, Charlie, what about the splurge gun?'

'Ssh.'

'Dandy Dan said take care of the splurge gun.' He bent down to pick up the weapon. The hood grabbed Doodle very roughly and yanked him into the street. 'You stupid idiot, Doodle. Watch your mouth, you fool.'

Another hood took Doodle's free arm and bundled him into the sedan. With a screech, they took off into the night.

The customers in the restaurant crawled out from under the tables, not quite sure what had happened. The violinist returned from the safety of the cheese counter and, as if nothing had happened, went straight into his very best version of 'O Sole Mio'.

Dobbs, the crooked accountant, was on the same list as Irving, only he didn't know it. He had been Fat Sam's accountant for as long as Fat Sam had run the rackets. He wasn't the fanciest accountant in the business. His office was his briefcase and his credentials were his two-year stretch in the State Pen. He hadn't thought of going straight ever since he was caught cheating in his accountancy examination finals. His one-room apartment was a mess, with empty packets of tea, his favourite weakness, strewn amongst the sheets of paper on which he'd totted up a million crooked sums. His dishonest living never worried him. He always slept well. Always, that is, unless he was interrupted—like tonight.

He first knew something was up when he heard the heavy feet of Bronx Charlie on the wooden staircase outside his door. He tried to open his eyes. This was difficult. He had been asleep for hours and his eyelids felt as if they were stapled together. He groped in the darkness for the switch on his bedside lamp. As it happened, this wasn't necessary. Bronx Charlie kicked open his bedroom door and the light from the hallway swept across Dobbs's bed. He blinked. His hair was a mess and his crumpled, dirty, blue and white striped pyjamas wouldn't have looked out of place in the garbage can. He blinked only once, or maybe twice, before the splurge gun Bronx Charlie was carrying burst into action and Dobbs was well and truly splurged against the brass railings of his bedhead. Bronx Charlie returned the way he had come, his feet thundering on the wooden stairs as he made his getaway.

6. A SPARKLE IN HIS EYE

Blousey thought she'd shaken him off. She stood on the kerb outside Pop Becker's bookstore and pulled on her gloves. But Bugsy was right behind her. Her face dropped. As she moved away, Bugsy quickly followed.

'Can I give you a lift?'

Blousey was determined to ignore him, but the offer of a lift was too tempting.

'You got a car?'

Bugsy couldn't lie. 'Er . . . no.'

Blousey was not impressed.

'So how you gonna give me a lift, buster? Stand me on a box?'

'I thought we'd share a cab.'

Blousey was even less impressed. 'Forget it, I don't share fares. I'm a lady. Furthermore, I'm broke.'

Blousey quickened her pace, and Bugsy had to run to keep up with her.

'Who said anything about sharing fares?'

'No?' Blousey was curious.

'Certainly not. I thought you'd pay.'

That was it. Not even if he turned out to be a Vanderbilt or a producer with the Ziegfeld Follies would she give him any more of her time.

Bugsy carried on undaunted. 'Well, let's walk, anyway. It's a nice night.'

Blousey splashed through a puddle and muttered under her breath. She was beginning to feel irritated by him.

'You shouldn't walk in the streets at night—it's dangerous.'

'We'll be all right. We've got your baseball bat.'

Blousey stopped dead in her tracks.

'Quit the *we*, pal. You mean *I'll* be all right.'

She started walking once more, this time even faster. Bugsy's little legs moved back and forth at twice their normal rate to catch up with her. He was beginning to puff as he spoke.

'Which way are you going?'

'Which way are *you* going?'

Bugsy thought for a moment. He was no brain surgeon, but his brain clicked away like two sharp-edged steel cubes. He wasn't really going anywhere special, but he'd made his mind up to tag along with her. He pointed in the direction that they were already walking. 'This way.'

He was wrong. Blousey did an immediate about turn.

'Then I'm going this way.'

Bugsy ran and caught her up. He tugged at the old leather bag, which seemed to be giving her a little trouble. She changed it from hand to hand, trying hard not to show that her arms felt like they were being pulled out of their sockets.

'Here, let me take that.'

'No, it's all right.'

Bugsy took the bag from her but she quickly snatched it back. Bugsy snatched once more. Maybe it was her aching arms, or maybe she was getting to like him. Either way she let him carry the bag. Bugsy wasn't overwhelmed by the compliment.

'Mama Mia! What have you got in here?'

'Just a few books.'

'You should start a library.'

'And you should shut your mouth.'

There was no way that Blousey was going to allow herself to lose a battle of words with this stranger. She was feeling pretty depressed after her wasted visit to the speakeasy, and not in the mood for a verbal ping-pong match with yet another New York wise guy. But the bag was heavy and he did have a sort of charm about him. Let's face it, she thought to herself, with a suit as baggy as he was wearing you'd need charm. It was true he'd certainly never make the best dressed top ten list in the *'Phoenix Tailor and Cutter Monthly'*, but then again, his eyes did sparkle a little—or seemed to whenever the street lamps flickered across his face. Or maybe his eyes were watering because his belt was too tight. No, she gave him the benefit of the doubt, it was a sparkle.

Bugsy took a deep breath as he changed hands on the bag. He thought he was in shape, but, not being prone to heavy work—or even light work—he never had much chance to find out how unfit he was. Bravely, he kept up his dialogue.

'Er . . . have you eaten?'

'Ever since I was a child.'

'Then how come you're so skinny, wisie?'

Blousey held in her tummy. 'I watch my weight.'

'Yeah, I do that when I'm broke too.'

It seemed to Blousey that Bugsy was getting the edge on her. Maybe she was tired.

'How about eating now?'

'No.'

'Why not?'

'I'm not hungry.'

It was Bugsy's turn to stop dead in his tracks. Any out of work dancer who had just lost out on the only audition she had that week, and then turned down a free meal ticket, had to be nuts.

'You're not hungry?'

'No, I'm starving.'

Blousey laughed for the first time. She wasn't kidding either. She hadn't eaten for two days. Well, except for a toasted bagel which she'd eaten very, very slowly and pretended each bite was a different dish. It had worked, too— she hadn't really felt hungry. Until Bugsy had mentioned food. That had done it. Her tummy gave her away. Lousy stomach, she thought, who's side are you on, anyway?

Bugsy smiled at her. She had dropped the 'I'll outwise you, wise guy' approach, and the new one suited her much better. She was kind of pretty, he thought, although she should never have worn that hat with the feather. She looked a little like Chief Sitting Bull. A few moments ago he would have told her so too. 'That hat don't do you justice, honey, you look like a cross between Chief Crazy Horse and last year's Thanksgiving turkey dinner.' But he didn't say it, because now they were friends, and he wasn't about to put her down while she was smiling at him. He kissed his finger and touched her on the nose. It was his way of passing on a little affection. He had done the very same thing three times tonight already. The hat-check girl, the cigarette girl—in fact, anybody who was kind enough to throw a smile in his direction. Blousey wasn't to know that. She smiled once more and they both moved in the direction of the drugstore.

Bugsy was pleased to buy her something to eat. After all, she looked like she needed a good meal. He was doing society a favour. There was just one snag. He had no money. Not a nickel. The contents of his pockets were made up exclusively of a ball of string, a jacket button and the used halves of tickets to the ball game. But that was the least of his worries. He was Bugsy Malone. He had a neat line in chat, and a suit he thought was a little smarter than people gave him credit for. And a sparkle in his eye. Like Blousey, he also used to think his eyes were watering because his belt was too tight. But some-one had called it a sparkle and he liked it. Yes—a sparkle in his eye and now a girl on his arm. Where he'd get the money to pay for the meal didn't even enter into his head. After all, he reasoned, even if he worried about it, it wouldn't have made him any richer.

7. FIZZY

Fizzy, the speakeasy's janitor, picked up a chair and turned it upside down to top of a table. Almost everyone had gone home, and he was cleaning up. On stage Raza-mataz and the rest of the band folded away their music. Fizzy whistled his bluesy song as he swept under the tables.

He had whistled that song for as long as he could remember. He hadn't been taught it. He hadn't heard it on the radio and it wasn't anything Razamataz had played. It belonged to Fizzy. Whenever anyone asked him, 'What's that song you're whistling, Fizzy?' he used to shrug his shoulders. People used to think it meant he didn't know the title. It had no title—except for Fizzy's Tune. Fizzy wasn't the type to say 'It's a little number I composed myself'—people probably wouldn't have believed him. Fizzy was a janitor and was meant to sweep up. That's how most people thought of him, because most people like to put folk in pigeon holes.

Fizzy had been to see Fat Sam as many times as he'd swept the speakeasy floor. Fat Sam always promised to give him an audition. 'If the kid can sing and dance, sure I'll see him,' he'd say, but somehow he never got around to it.

Out of the door that led to the changing rooms came two chorus girls—Bangles and Tillie. Bangles was a little plumper than the rest of the girls and chewed gum until her face muscles ached. She also talked a lot, which, all things considered, was very unfair on her jaw—and on the ears of whoever was nearby. It's not untrue to say that the other girls tended to avoid Bangles whenever they could. Tillie had been caught on the way out and was visibly suffering from the non-stop chatter that was dribbling out of Bangles' mouth.

Fizzy stopped sweeping long enough to say goodnight to the two girls. He brushed his dirty hands down the front of his dungarees and pecked them both on the cheek. ' 'Bye, Bangles, 'bye, Tillie. Take it easy now.'

' 'Night, Fizzy.'

The rest of the girls trooped out, saying goodnight to Fizzy and Razamataz as they went. Fizzy picked up a bucket and mop. He hummed his tune and swished the water round and round in time with the bluesy beat. Just then, Fat Sam burst through the door from his office. Fizzy never wasted an opportunity to ask for an audition and this time was as good as any. But Fat Sam was obviously preoccupied. He gave Fizzy as much time as he did the wooden hat-rack by the exit door. He didn't mean to be nasty. It was just that he had a lot on his mind right now, and tap dancing janitors were as important to him as yesterday's papers.

Knuckles helped Sam into his overcoat and faithfully

brushed him down with a brush he kept in his inside pocket. His task completed, he promptly cracked the knuckles of his left hand—like a full stop at the end of a sentence.

This habit irritated Fat Sam no end. He would shout at Knuckles to stop it. And the more Fat Sam shouted, the more nervous Knuckles would get. And the more nervous he got, the more he'd crack his knuckles—and consequently Fat Sam shouted at him even more. It was a strange cycle, a confused roundabout that poor old Knuckles had no way of jumping off.

He pressed his fist into his hand and the bones wiggled together to let out that unmistakable sound like a nut yielding to a nut-cracker.

'Don't do that, Knuckles.'

'But it's how I got my name, Boss.'

'Well, knock it off, else change your name.'

Knuckles bowed his head and nervously put his arms behind his back out of harm's way. Fat Sam was growing impatient. He stalked up and down flexing his fingers and shooting out his arms to expose the neat starched shirt cuffs. He did it without thinking. Just as Knuckles clicked at his hands. Fat Sam shouted impatiently in the direction of the dressing room, 'Tallulah, are you ready? How much longer you want us to wait?'

Tallulah wasn't about to be hurried. She was the star of the Fat Sam Show and nobody hurried her. She'd hurried and bustled for too long and now she was taking things a little easier. Her tired, lazy voice drifted down the stairs.

'Coming, honey. You don't want me looking a mess, do you?'

Fat Sam threw his hands into the air, and paced the floor, his shoes echoing on the shiny wooden floor boards. He was uneasy. Knuckles watched his boss carefully, knowing that something was up but not daring to interfere. Without thinking, he cracked his knuckles in sympathy with what Fat Sam was thinking. Sam scowled at him with such venom that no words were necessary. Knuckles put his hands in his pockets.

'Sorry, Boss. It kind of . . . slipped out.'

Meanwhile, Fizzy had plucked up enough courage to speak.

'Er . . . Mr Stacetto, about the audition . . .'

Fat Sam looked at him for the first time. He wasn't unkind. He liked Fizzy and if there was ever enough time —which there wasn't—he would have given him a chance. He put his friendly, podgy hand on Fizzy's shoulder.

'Later, Fizzy. I'm busy right now . . . keep practising, son. Keep practising.' Tallulah appeared at the top of the stairs. She didn't look any the better for all her make-up repair, but she felt better. She always felt better when she kept Fat Sam waiting. She was probably the only person living who could get away with it, and she knew it.

'You spend more time prettying yourself up than there is time in the day,' grumbled Sam.

Tallulah's reply was quick.

'Listen, honey, if I didn't look this good you wouldn't give me the time of day.'

Sam didn't like getting the worst of this verbal sword fence.

'I'll see you in the car,' he muttered, heading for the door.

Tallulah paused to drop a soft goodnight kiss on the top of Fizzy's head as she followed Sam out.

' 'Night, Fizzy.'

Fizzy sighed, and picked up his broom again. As he swept, his broom seemed to make the rhythmic sound of a drummer's brush on the side drum. Softly, all alone in the empty, dimly lit speakeasy, Fizzy began to sing. It wasn't a happy song. Not the song you sing when you're in the bath. It was a sad, gritty song about not being given a chance, about being passed over, about being taken for granted like the tables and chairs around him. Fizzy turned as he sang and opened a small broom cupboard under the stairs. He reached inside and took out a parcel wrapped in a blue chequered duster. Slowly he unwrapped a pair of spanking new tap shoes. The boots he was wearing were worn out and shabby—but not these shoes. They were made of the finest, crispest, brown and cream leather, with hand stitching and neat bows. They had cost Fizzy ten weeks' wages but they were worth every cent. The leather soles had never been trodden on. The shiny metal plates had never seen a scratch. Fizzy was the greatest tap dancer on earth, he always said. But it wasn't really on earth, because on earth he couldn't dance a step. It was in his imagination. Somewhere up there in a cloudy, never-never land where dreamers live.

As he sang his lonely song, he heard a noise in the upstairs corridor. His expression changed to a sheepish grin as he saw Velma, the black girl dancer, coming down the stairs. Velma took the situation in at once. She said nothing, but she dropped her coat on the ground and began to dance for Fizzy. As they say in show business, Velma could dance a bit—which was an understatement, because Velma could dance a lot. She glided amongst the tables, her feet scarcely making contact with the floor. If Sam had ever seen Fizzy and Velma's secret double act he'd have made them the Grand Slam's star attraction. But it was an act that no one ever saw, except the tables and chairs who silently partnered them on the speakeasy floor.

8. NO COMMENT

The newspapers hit the streets late that night. It had been what's called a 'no-news' night, until the sinister splurge guns had burst into action and made the headlines their own. Every editor in town was glad of it. *The Record* had been running as its lead story an item on a movie star's fifth husband, whilst *The News* was occupied, as it had been for three no-news nights, with the evergreen rise in taxes. They had all stopped their late issues and reset their front pages. The size of the type in *The Record* was enormous. It had been a little bigger when world war was declared, but not much. '*New Weapon For Mobsters!*' it screamed, and followed up with six whole columns of editorial. *The News* tried a well-trusted formula for their headline: '*New Gang War Flares*' flashed across their printing rollers and ended up in neat, string-tied bundles.

One of these bundles was thrown on to the sidewalk on East 6th Street. The paper boy cut the string with his penknife and lifted the papers on to his knee. He flipped the top copy off the bundle. The ink was still wet and he touched his forehead with his blackened thumb as he read the headline, 'New Weapon Revealed'. He hadn't had a break like that in weeks. He read the article and then began to shout at the top of his voice. 'New weapon revealed. Read all about it. Gang war flares. Read all about it. New weapon revealed . . .' He repeated his sales pitch until he was hoarse. It didn't bother him—tonight he would sell out.

At the International Press Exchange, the row of glass-fronted phone booths were jammed with newsmen screaming their messages to news desks in faraway places. The Frenchman in the first booth was the most emotional. He also had his suitcase with him. He was obviously taking no chances, and would be on the next boat home if things got out of hand. The next booth was occupied by a German who spat his story into the phone and punctuated his sentences with sharp clicks of his heels. Next to him, an Indian gentleman in a turban shouted hurriedly into his phone, interspersing his story with worried glances over his shoulder in case the situation worsened. The Japanese journalist was quite carried away with his version of the story. He emphasised his description of the splurge guns with demonstrative karate chops on the telephone directories. The Englishman next door was calm and collected on the surface, but was expressing alarm with as much emotion as his stiff upper lip would allow. He spoke rather than shouted into the receiver. 'There's been a frightfully bad show here in America, chaps, and this time the Yanks have gone too far. What's more, what I have to tell you is certainly not cricket . . .'

Cricket it certainly wasn't. The morse code tappers worked overtime that night as the message flashed across the headlines of the world. 'Official: The Splurge Gun'.

Back in New York, the local radio news announcer interrupted, for the umpteenth time, the programme of music that traditionally occupied Friday night. The Roscoe Ravelo Combo were getting a little fed up with having their repertoire interrupted. Roscoe himself had thrown his baton at the wall at the last announcement, and with this interruption he let his Latin temperament get the

33

better of him and promptly snapped the baton in two across his knee. The news announcer rushed on.

'We interrupt Roscoe Ravelo's delightful music to bring you a further bulletin on developments in the latest outbreak of hoodlum gang warfare. Police now officially state that the new weapon of devious foreign manufacture known as the "splurge gun" is now being widely used by the mobster gangs. We interrupt our interruption to go straight over to our reporter, Seymour Scoop, who is on the spot at the latest splurging . . .'

The alleyway where Roxy had been so effectively splurged was filled with newsmen. As police officers tried to keep the inquiring journalists under control, flashing camera bulbs lit up the already electric atmosphere. Seymour Scoop, the radio station's ace reporter, jostled to the front and pushed his microphone in front of Lieutenant O'Dreary, the second in command of the police investigation team. His superior, Captain Smolsky, was busy shouting out instructions to his officers.

'Have you located the splurge gun yet, Lieutenant?'

O'Dreary, who had not been the brightest of cadets at the police academy, tried to give the impression he was in control. He said, 'I'm afraid I can't answer that.'

'You're not at liberty to say?' probed Seymour Scoop.

'No. I don't have the answer.'

It was the truth. And not only in this investigation, either. O'Dreary hadn't the answer to any questions.

Another journalist managed to push the resourceful Scoop out of the limelight and shot in a question of his own. 'Have you located the source, Lieutenant?'

The only source O'Dreary knew about was the ketchup he put on his hamburgers. He kept his dignity. 'Er . . . I'm not at liberty to say. You'll have to ask Captain Smolsky that question . . .'

As if on cue, the burly Smolsky pushed his way through the crowd. He wore a dirty, beige-coloured trench coat that was belted tightly at the waist. He chewed on a toothpick and also gave the impression that he knew everything but would say nothing, which was roughly the opposite of the truth. He talked out of the corner of his mouth and his top lip curled up as he did so.

'O.K., O'Dreary, break this crowd up.'

Scoop regained his front position and put in his question. 'Seymour Scoop, RTZ Radio, Captain Smolsky. Captain Smolsky, have you located the splurge gun yet, sir?'

'No comment.'

'Have you located the source?' Scoop's rival beat him to his second question.

'No comment.'

'Is it true, Captain Smolsky, that the gun is being used by only one gang?'

'No comment.'

At this point, O'Dreary appeared with his boss's evening snack. He handed the thick sandwich over the heads of the crowd.

'I fixed you a pastrami sandwich, Chief. Is that O.K.?'

Captain Smolsky was as deaf to this question as he had been to the others. He treated it in the same way.

'No comment.'

The flash bulbs dazzled his eyes as Smolsky's ruddy face shared the picture with a pastrami and rye sandwich.

9. EIGHT BANANA BOOZLES

The barlady in the drugstore yawned once more. She looked up at the clock. It said 2 a.m. and she yawned yet again and cleared her throat, as if to point out the fact. Across the other side of the drugstore, in a booth of their own, were Bugsy and Blousey. As far as the barlady was concerned they had outstayed their welcome. She wasn't the friendliest of souls at the best of times, and when she missed her beauty sleep she got even meaner. Beauty sleep was a joke anyway. She had the kind of face that needed a personality behind it. It was the kind of face what girls call plain, and guys call the back end of a down-town bus. She was built like a Mac truck, and her shoulders would have done credit to an all-in wrestler.

She cleaned her counter for maybe the hundredth time. Bugsy and Blousey hadn't taken any notice. They were too busy talking to one another. On the table of their booth was a litter of empty plates and banana sundae glasses. They had eaten well.

'Are you going back to the speakeasy tomorrow?' Bugsy asked.

'It depends. I'm going to try my luck at the Bijoux Theatre. They're auditioning.'

Bugsy looked up from his drink. He furrowed his brow a little. 'Lena Marrelli's show?'

'She's walked out. They're looking for a replacement.'

Bugsy nodded. He knew that Lena Marrelli walked out of that show four times a week and everyone except Blousey knew that she always came back. It was all part of being a star. You stamped your feet, tossed your head in the air and, in a blur of mink, vanished out of the stage door. Bugsy knew they were auditioning for supporting acts, but he wasn't going to let on to Blousey. It was nicer being nice, and she'd already had one disappointment that night. He changed the subject slightly.

'How long have you wanted to be a singer?'

'Since I was a kid, I guess. Actually, I don't want just to be a singer and a dancer, I wanna be a movie-star, in Hollywood.'

Bugsy smiled into his sundae. He stirred at the pink drink with his straw. He hoped she hadn't seen him smile —but she had.

'What's so funny?'

Bugsy wasn't quite sure whether to be honest or tactful. He decided on the latter. It seemed a little more charming, and the sparkle in his eye was working overtime. 'I don't know. It's just that there used to be a time when people were happy to be railway engineers or nurses or something.'

Blousey was annoyed. She wasn't over-ambitious, but it smarted when she met someone so complacent it made her seem so.

'Don't you want to be anybody?'

He shrugged his shoulders and smiled.

'No, I'm happy being me.'

He had put her down without really meaning to. She

was irritated at first, but then she smiled. She was beginning to find him interesting. 'And what do you do?'

'Oh, this and that.'

'Oh, crooked, huh?'

'No, in between—walking the line, trying hard not to fall either side.'

It was true enough. He'd spent his life on the Lower East Side and it was a lot harder keeping on the straight and narrow than going crooked. With an Irish father and an Italian mother he had naturally grown up somewhat confused. He couldn't see his future as a spaghetti waiter in a restaurant or as a clerk at City Hall, filling in endless forms. So he'd drifted from this to that. Never very crooked, not always completely honest. But generally to do with boxing, his great love.

'But what do you do for money?' Blousey asked.

'I find fighters . . . boxers.'

'Oh really?'

'I used to fight myself.'

'You did? How good were you?'

Bugsy put on a mock voice. 'I could have been a contender.'

It was true—in a way. He could have been a contender but he would never have made champion. He had a lot of style. He was very quick and made his opponents look slow and awkward. For a round or so, that is. After that he was about as tough as a cotton-wool ball, and one punch was generally enough to send him on the way back to the dressing room, usually on a stretcher. They'd slap his face and get out the smelling salts and he'd come round and say he never saw the punch. He'd also say he'd never do it again. But he always did, until one day he really woke up and called it a day. He looked at some of the other fighters and realised how much better he looked without cauliflower ears and a nose that spread itself halfway across his face and nearly shook hands with an ear. It had really saddened him at the time, but he knew if he carried on, the only title he'd end up with would be 'bum of the month'.

Blousey was very interested. 'You could have been a contender?'

'Sure. But for a few things.'

'Like what?'

37

'Oh, like a glass jaw, jelly legs, no stamina and most of all . . . I got scared.'

'Some contender.'

They both laughed. Blousey had reached the bottom of her glass and there was a small silence for a while.

'Do you want another drink in there?'

'No, thanks, I've had enough.'

Bugsy was persistent. A lot more persistent than he ought to have been, considering he was broke. 'Come on.'

'I thought you didn't have any money.'

'I haven't.'

'You haven't? Then how are we gonna . . . ?'

'Don't worry. I'll think of something.'

Bugsy had no idea how he was going to pay, but that bridge wasn't to come for five minutes or more, so he saw no reason to worry about crossing it now. With great bravado, he twisted in his seat to face the sour-faced lady. 'Two more drinks, please.'

The barlady had had enough. She threw her cleaning cloth into the sink, leaned on one muscular arm and said, 'Look, pal. The food counter's closed, the bar's closed, my eyes are closing—in fact, the whole joint's closed.'

Blousey wasn't about to cause an argument. She smiled politely at the ogre in the white cap.

'I didn't want one, anyway.'

Bugsy turned to Blousey and stretched out to touch her hand. They began to sing to each other. This was too much for the giantess behind the counter. She screamed at them, 'Knock it off, will yuh? What do you think this joint is—some kind of Hollywood musical?'

Bugsy and Blousey knew they had outstayed their welcome. Bugsy said, 'Let's go,' and helped Blousey into her coat.

Without saying another word, he slipped into the phone booth in the corner of the drugstore. He pulled the door closed. The barlady glowered at Blousey, who blushed.

Bugsy dialled a number and spoke very quietly into the mouthpiece. 'Hello, operator? Could you test this line, please? I believe we have a fault. It's Columbus 4181. Thank you.'

Bugsy winked at Blousey as he went up to the counter to pay. She looked scared. Bugsy put his hand deep into his pocket to pull out his money. 'How much do I owe you?' he inquired politely. The barlady, her face as sullen as ever, began to add up the bill on her scribble pad. She read out the damage.

'Eight Banana Boozles, with double ice-cream, three Beef Spitfires, two cream Arizona doughnuts and a Salami Special. Four dollars, eighty cents.' She tore off the page from the pad with a sharp flick of her wrist. Bugsy fumbled in his seemingly bottomless pocket for his wallet. Blousey looked even more scared and the barlady even more suspicious. At that moment, the phone in the booth rang. The barlady excused herself and went to answer the operator's call that Bugsy had set up. She pulled the door closed behind her, and as she sat down on the stool Bugsy crept quietly up to the booth. He could hear her muffled voice through the glass.

'Yes, this is Columbus 4181. No, I didn't ask to have the line tested. Are you sure you have the right line?'

Bugsy took the broom that was lying by the side of the counter and threaded it through the large brass handles on the booth door. The barlady put the phone down immediately, and, like a saucepan of milk boiling over, erupted. She suddenly realised she'd been conned and began frantically to rattle the doors, which were securely held by her own broom. The bad language she poured out ricocheted around the closed booth. Bugsy and Blousey didn't hear her, that was for sure. They had quietly slipped out of the main door long ago.

10. SMOLSKY AND O'DREARY

The sunlight streamed through the window of Mama Lugini's restaurant. The customers had long gone home, but for the police it was business as usual. Captain Smolsky belted up his coat, more out of habit than because of the cold, and paced the floor. The waiter who had seen the splurging said nothing. He watched the proceedings, almost too frightened to speak. Smolsky spat out questions.

'Five guys there were, you say?'

The waiter nodded.

'How about you? What did you see?'

The cop fired his question in the direction of the violinist, who still had his violin tucked under his chin. He had probably forgotten it was there.

'Nuttink. I see nuttink.'

'You must have seen something—you were playing when they broke the window, weren't you?'

'Yes.'

'You was playing when they fired the guns, weren't you?'

'Yes.'

'Then you must have seen something.'

Sheepishly, the violinist owned up to his cowardice. Anyway, he thought, he was a musician, and at three dollars fifty a night he wasn't required to be a hero.

Smolsky turned to Lieutenant O'Dreary, who was on his knees under one of the tables. He had a box of face powder beside him and was dusting the floor where the gun had been dropped by Doodle.

Smolsky picked up a bentwood chair, turned it around and sat astride it like a rodeo rider. His scalp itched from the sweat that trickled down his neck. He scratched at it hard. It made a nasty rasping sound in his head like sandpaper on a block of wood. True, there were those who thought that a block of wood was a good description of the grey matter between Smolsky's ears. He had probably been single-handedly responsible for all those Polish jokes at Headquarters. His Polish immigrant father had had high expectations of him but he had never quite made it to brain surgeon, as his family expected. On the other hand, he could still make President of the United States. Smolsky Senior would often tell his elderly chess partners this on the back step. It was the American dream after all—from poor boy to the highest office in the land. He'd been told it was possible when he filled in his immigration forms after getting off the boat at Ellis Island.

Smolsky Senior still hoped, and Smolsky Junior would never douse these hopes. He would say, 'Sure, Pappa,

40

only fifty more arrests to go and I could be Commissioner. And after that . . . who knows.'

The truth was that if Smolsky could make even one arrest they'd run a headline in the Police Gazette proclaiming a miracle. Not that he hadn't tried. He would read his detective manuals and the Private Eye magazines from cover to cover, watch the movies—anything to get a teeny, weeny inkling of how to track down his man, trap him, arrest him and lock him in a cell. So far, sad to say, it hadn't worked. His Lieutenant, O'Dreary, wasn't much better. If one week Headquarters had a rest from Polish jokes, O'Dreary's antics would guarantee an outbreak of conversations beginning, 'Have you heard the one about the Irishman who . . .' He was the classic Bronx flatfoot who had been promoted for fear of what he might get up to if left alone to patrol the sidewalks. They made a fine team all right.

O'Dreary brushed away at the dusting powder on the floor. He suddenly let out a small but confident exclamation. 'Aha!'

Smolsky stopped scratching his head and looked down. 'What can you see?'

'A gun, Captain!'

Smolsky couldn't contain himself. He jumped up and crouched close to the powder on the floor, which revealed the outline of the gun that Doodle had so carelessly dropped. He whispered in excitement, 'Yeah, O'Dreary. I know it's a gun. But what kind of a gun?'

O'Dreary looked once again at his work of art. This time he was a little puzzled. His police examination marks had been even lower than Smolsky's. [The lowest two in history, it was rumoured, but no one had let on for fear of making O'Malley's Book of World Records.] He looked hard at the shape of the gun, like a fortune teller looking into a cup of tealeaves.

Smolsky asked him again. 'Well, what kind of a gun, O'Dreary?'

The floppy skin of O'Dreary's furrowed brow unfolded as his face changed from puzzled to pleased. 'A *big* gun, Captain?' he ventured.

'You great dumb knucklehead! You've been brushing away at that powder for an hour and a half and all you can tell me is that it's a big gun—you noodle-brained Irish stewpot!'

Smolsky had suffered from insults enough as a kid and he enjoyed getting his own back on O'Dreary. O'Dreary, on the other hand, couldn't get his own back on anyone. He was one of those unfortunate people who were at the end of the line. All he could do to get even was to put too many sugars in Smolsky's coffee, or too much mustard on his hot dog. To most people, that wouldn't seem much, but O'Dreary was a simple person and his pleasures came easy. Nevertheless, Smolsky whipped off his hat and belted it across O'Dreary's head. O'Dreary covered himself with his arms, pretending that it hurt, but he was only kidding. Smolsky liked to hit O'Dreary, but what he didn't know was that O'Dreary didn't mind. If Smolsky had known that, it would have annoyed him even more.

II. DANDY DAN

The rider of the grey polo pony pulled his mount sharply to one side to avoid an almost certain head-on collision. The white ball, sitting innocently beneath the churning hooves, needn't have looked so smug—as a wooden polo mallet swung through an arc and hit it full in the face. It jumped into the air, and the grass divot it had been hiding behind was yanked out by its roots and sent flying eight feet away. The ball travelled for some distance, and the opposing player was unable to turn his horse quickly enough to stop it bounce—and finally trickle across the white goal line. A few spectators applauded the goal with some 'Well done's', and 'A chukkha well won, fellows', and the other various mechanical outbursts that accompany any sporting congratulations.

Off the field of play, a string quartet sat on a neatly manicured lawn, playing as enthusiastically as they would have done on any concert platform. They wore full evening dress and seemed quite unconcerned about the ridiculousness of their setting as they belted out their attempt at Mozart amongst the flowering bushes. Their heads swayed in unison, as they tried to avoid the lawn sprinkler which regularly sprayed an impromtu shower across the cellist. This interruption, however, had little or no effect on their playing.

Dandy Dan's mansion was situated a good hour's drive from the city. It was a typical product of the newer American fortunes that sprinkled their great brick and iron monstrosities around the perimeter of New York in the early nineteen twenties. It was a copy of a famous seat of European aristocracy. Dandy Dan was never quite sure if it was English or French—he'd been shown a magazine and had pointed at one of the pictures that caught his eye. His architects and builders had simply gone ahead and built it for him.

On the other side of Dandy Dan's estate, a bike sedan pulled to a halt on the loose gravel with a crunching sound. Bronx Charlie was the first to get out. He always sat up front with the driver, and when Dandy Dan wasn't around, Bronx Charlie was number one man in the gang. Out of the back of the vehicle climbed Shoulders, Yonkers, Benny Lee, Doodle and Laughing Boy. Straightening their baggy jackets and shooting their cuffs as they walked, they made their way around a lily pond and across a small ornamental stone bridge. Doodle stopped for a while and absentmindedly threw a stone into the pond. It disturbed the neat, floating lilies and a sleeping duck, which scampered out of the reeds, more surprised than annoyed. The other hoods stopped and looked back. For some reason, Doodle never seemed to fit in Dan's gang. He was one of those people who always look like they don't belong. Doodle was the black sheep of Dandy Dan's gang. His suit wasn't quite up to the tailored excellence of the other hoods. He was a little crumpled around the places where the others boasted a knife-edge crease. It is true to say that he resembled a potato sack more than a tailor's dummy. He wore very thick glasses that perched, like the bottoms of milk bottles, on the end of his nose. The wire that held them together had pinched his nose for so many years that it had resulted in a permanent red mark across the bridge, and a rather squeaky nasal voice. He quickened his step to catch up with the others. He was quite happy to be one of the Dandy Dan gang and felt more at home than he ought to have.

Outside the house, the hoods were met by an immaculate butler, who waited for them to gather before showing them in. They followed him along a mahogany-panelled corridor and turned the corner into a large conservatory. The atmosphere was damp and hot, and they all felt a little uncomfortable amongst the ferns and Russian vines. The butler threw them all a disapproving look as he left, clearing his throat and pointing to their hats. Bronx Charlie whipped his from his head and the rest followed suit. They twirled the brims nervously between their fingers, afraid to talk and a little overawed by the grandeur of the surroundings.

Out on the polo field, a groom grappled with Dandy Dan's pony as he prepared to lead it away. The pony's head bobbed up and down, and it took the featherweight groom with it, raising him off the ground by a good six inches. Dandy Dan dismounted. He was a little clumsy and his hand-made riding boot got caught in the stirrup. But Dan kept his head, as befitted a gentleman who had devoted a lifetime to extravagant exhibitions of showy cool. His polo clothes were, of course, immaculate. After all, there were no errors in Dandy Dan's wardrobe. He chose his clothes with as much care as he used in choosing his tactics for outwitting Fat Sam. As he jumped on to the grass, the butler came up and stood there silently. Dan caught sight of him out of the corner of his eye.

'Yes, Johnson?'

'There's a Mr Bronx Charlie and company to see you, sir. They're waiting in the conservatory.'

Johnson spoke with a neat and precise English accent that sounded as if it would have been more at home on the playing fields of Eton than on the polo field of this Long Island mansion. Dan pushed his cap off his forehead and dabbed his moist brow with a monogrammed silk handkerchief.

'I'll be right in.' His reply was sharp but courteous. Johnson had served the crowned heads of Europe and he had the unfortunate habit of frequently reminding people of the fact. Naturally, he wasn't overfond of the visitors to Dan's house. Not his sort of people at all. But he'd taken the post for a while until he was summoned to higher places.

At that moment, a very attractive blonde girl with a pale, colourless face and a bright colourful jacket rode in on another pony. She balanced her polo stick on her finger and pulled her face into a bored expression that her extremely pretty features really didn't deserve. 'Ain't you gonna play no more, honey?' she drawled.

Dan looked up at her and furrowed his dark eyebrows into a tight knot.

'Later, my rose, later.' He sounded like a farmer talking to a loved and trusty dog.

The girl pouted her pretty lips even more, and, pulling at her pony's reins, briskly rode back to continue the game.

Dandy Dan took a clothesbrush from the silver tray Johnson was carrying and stiffly brushed a few specks of dust from his shoulders. He threw the brush at the butler and it landed in the tray with a loud clang. Johnson didn't even blink. His eyelids drooped a little and his eyeballs stared impassively at Dandy Dan as he bounded up the white stone steps into the house. A few more months, he thought to himself, and another post was bound to crop up. Bound to.

The hoods clicked their heels to attention as Dandy Dan entered the tall glass conservatory. They looked even more apprehensive than when they'd first arrived. The humidity, mixed with their nerves, was bringing out little beads of sweat on their foreheads. The sun was glinting through the thousands of small panes of glass and made the plants and flowers look quite beautiful. Dan paced up and down.

'Hi, boys. O.K., relax. Well, guys, I'd like to take this opportunity of thanking you for your work so far. Everything's gone swell, just swell.'

The faces of the hoods changed immediately, and in their relief they smiled at one another rather more broadly than was necessary. Bronx Charlie, the spokesman for the group, offered a reply.

'Gee, thanks, Boss.'

Dandy Dan picked up a large pair of metal rose pruning shears and waved them rather menacingly in the air. The gang watched in silence as he began to snip at the prickly stems of the rose bush climbing up the great iron centre column that supported the domed glass roof. The hoods blinked as the metal tool cut off the roses' life lines. Dan was silent. The beads of sweat started to dribble down the hoods' foreheads again. Dan turned with the cut flowers in his hands, and proceeded to hand them to the gang members almost like a general decorating his troops after a victory. One by one they took their flowers, and received a hearty handshake.

'Bronx Charlie . . . Laughing Boy . . . Shoulders . . . Yonkers . . . Benny Lee,' Dan smiled, but strangely, he made a point of missing Doodle, who stood sandwiched between Shoulders and Yonkers. Doodle stood there a little surprised. He stared down at his empty hand and was not quite sure why he'd been left out. He gulped heavily, and the sweat beads on his forehead multiplied ten fold as he summoned the necessary courage that would allow him to cough up a few words.

Dan continued his speech of praise for the rest of the gang.

'Any moment now, Fat Sam will be crawling on his knees to me.'

They all nodded in agreement, except for Doodle who was still a little behind the others. He spoke. 'What about my flower, Boss?'

Dan made a point of ignoring Doodle's squeaky plea. But the rest of the gang were well aware of what was happening, and already they were eyeing Doodle with more than a little pity. Dan said, 'Yes, soon all Fat Sam will have is the suit he stands up in and a suitcase full of memories.'

Doodle cleared his throat and tried again. 'Er . . . I don't have a flower, Boss.'

This time his voice was louder.

Dan said nothing. Instead, he put down the nasty-looking shears and picked up a silver hand-bell. He shook it without taking his stare away from Doodle. The other hoods took their cue from the ringing bell and moved away from Doodle, who was left standing alone. Unsure of what to do, he looked at his leader and then at the faces of his fellow hoods.

46

'Boss? What's going on here? I don't understand . . .'

He didn't understand, but he was the only person standing in that glass conservatory who didn't. It was so evident what was going to happen that even the Russian vines could have told him—if they spoke English. The English butler, who, incidentally, was certain he was the only person who could speak English, came in with a tray of immaculate custard pies. He put them down on a bamboo cane table and made a somewhat showy exit backwards through the doors. Dandy Dan took a pie from the tray and turned to Doodle.

'You goofed, Doodle. You dropped the gun. I don't allow mistakes in this outfit. 'Cause mistakes put us all in the caboose—and Sing Sing ain't my style.'

Doodle finally got the message. He was dumb, but the coin had dropped and he was aware of his predicament for the first time. He sweated so much that his spectacles steamed up.

Taking their cue from Dandy Dan, the other hoods each took a custard pie from the tray. They hadn't taken any orders to do so, it was an unsaid thing between them. Dandy Dan had told them everything by his disapproving, darting eyes that stared at Doodle, dissecting him limb by limb. They all advanced towards Doodle, who started to back away. He let out a last, desperate squeak.

'No, Boss, not that. I didn't mean to drop the gun, honest I didn't. It just kind of slipped out of my hands . . . Any guy can make a mistake.'

He kicked over a potted plant as he made his clumsy retreat. Dan was in no mood to trade words with Doodle. He spat out the final judgement with great contempt.

'Button your lip, Doodle. You're all washed up.'

Doodle was flabbergasted.

'But, Boss—give a guy a break, won't you?'

He needn't have bothered. Dandy Dan had never given anybody a break in his life. A sagging green creeper almost strangled Doodle as he stepped backwards in his desperation to escape. He tugged at the leafy noose, but it was unnecessary because at that moment the gang let fly with their custard missiles. They threw with enormous gusto and great accuracy. Doodle didn't stand a chance. He looked a neat, bespectacled sight as he lay there, splurged from head to foot, among the Russian vines and climbing hydrangeas.

12. NEXT!

A viking helmet is never very comfortable and this one weighed very heavily on the head of the Brooklyn soprano whose voice echoed to the empty gallery of the Bijoux Theatre. She clasped herself in a strange self-embrace as she screeched out her song. The brass breastplate she was squeezed into might have had something to do with her agonised tone, as her lips trembled and her tongue wobbled for all it was worth at the back of her throat.

'Velia! Oh, Velia, the witch of the wood . . .'

She had the kind of voice that breaks wineglasses and eardrums. It wasn't a dreadful voice, but it would be fair to say that it was in the no man's land somewhere between pretty terrible and awful. But she had guts. With a voice that bad, you need guts. She was what music teachers call a tryer. She ploughed into the second verse of her song unaware of the special kind of torture she was inflicting on her audience.

The occasion was the audition session for Lena Marrelli's Show. Lena had stormed out, as she had done a thousand times, and her producer, Oscar De Velt, had said it was the last time she would walk out on him. He had said that before, of course—almost as many times as Lena had abandoned the show.

'Let her go,' he'd said. 'I don't need her.' Oscar De Velt had been putting on Broadway shows when Lena Marrelli was in pig-tails. She still was in pig-tails, but he always omitted this fact from his thoughts. Her floppy red ringlets and precocious talent had paid for his silk shirts and velveteen jackets and his apartment overlooking Central Park for too long for him to see things clearly. Every time she quit, he set up a new casting session. Amongst the pros it was regarded as a bore and not to be taken seriously. But to the hopefuls, the first timers in New York, the dreamers, the ones that didn't know the ropes, it was their big chance.

Oscar De Velt, dressed like every Broadway producer, went through the charade of pretending to look for new talent. Slumped in the third row of the stalls, his arm dangling over the back of the seat and his hand-stitched boots propped up on the row in front, he shouted at the acts to be auditioned. He had a rather nasty, smart but spotty secretary who had even more disregard for personal feelings than he did. She would rebuke the cracked sopranos and squeaky tenors with a mouthful of abuse that sent many a hopeful packing back to their home town.

'Next!'

That evil word that says so much to the plucky, but talentless, auditioner. It may only be a little word, but it can be interpreted a million different ways. 'Next' could mean, 'Thank you very much, you are extremely talented and will surely go far, only you're just a teeny bit tall for us.' On the other hand, it could mean, 'Get off the stage quickly—your ears stick out, your voice sounds like a cat who's caught his tail in the door, your knees are as bandy as a viola player's and you'd do a great service to showbusiness by taking a job in a laundry.'

'Next!' Oscar De Velt yelled once more. This time, a conjurer came out and brushed down his dress suit rather too many times and took immense pains to put up the stand for his tricks. The metal legs were a little wobbly to begin with, but he tried to hide his nerves by persevering with the troublesome brass joints. The long line of auditioners waited impatiently for their brief chance for Broadway immortality. The conjurer cleared his throat most politely and walked to the footlights to deliver his hopeful showbusiness broadside.

'Good evening. I am the Great Marbini, illusionist to kings. I have been privileged to have obtained second billing at theatres in Missouri, Polar Bluff and Norfolk, Nebraska, and will now perform for you a trick only before seen by the crowned heads of Europe. I will produce from this hat not one rabbit, not two rabbits, but *three* rabbits.' As he spoke, he indicated on his fingers the rabbits he hoped to pluck out of the hat. This proud boast met with an expansive yawn from the producer and a bored stare from his assistant. Oscar De Velt shouted, 'Next! Next! Next!' to each of the conjurer's three rabbits and the conjurer disappeared from the stage as quickly as only an illusionist could.

Blousey waited nervously in the long audition queue with Bugsy. She handed him her mirror, which he held up for her whilst she fixed her make-up.

'I wish they'd hurry up. I get so nervous waiting.'

'Quit worrying, will you,' Bugsy said. He was beginning to feel nervous himself.

'I didn't figure on this many people.' Blousey bit on her bottom lip as she craned her neck in search of the end of the queue, which seemed to go on forever.

'Oh, they're all jugglers and magicians by the look of it. Don't worry. You've got no competition. You'll walk it, believe me.'

Blousey was in no mood to be calmed down. The make-believe butterflies in her tummy fluttered about trying to get out. She pressed her lips together to spread the lipstick evenly, and tucked a loose hair into her feathered skull cap.

'How do I look?'

Bugsy gave the same answer as he had given a dozen times. 'Fine.'

'I look a wreck.' She was getting more nervous.

'You look swell.'

'Honest?'

Bugsy nodded, at last he seemed to be getting somewhere. 'Honest.'

'Cross your heart?'

'Cross my heart. You look beautiful.'

He kissed his finger and touched her on the nose. She forgot her butterflies and smiled for the first time.

Auditioning was never easy in such surroundings, and the constant toing and froing of the men who were moving the props didn't help either. A four girl dancing group with rather too-plump thighs did a high kicking number that finished with them ploughing through the scenery.

Oscar De Velt put his head in his hands and a muffled 'Next' seemed to come out.

A ventriloquist came forward and the wooden dummy she was holding seemed to realise they were on to a loser before his operator did.

'I guppose goo are gundering gwy I'm here tonight?'

The lady ventriloquist exposed her dentures. True, her lips didn't move but, there again, the words didn't come out all that clearly either. She replied to the dummy, whose wooden head swivelled on its stick and whose bottom jaw flapped up and down, squeaking as it did so.

'Garen't goo going to gask me gow I gam?'

'Well, how are you, Clarence?'

'Gon't gask. I feel gerrible.'

'Gnext!' The producer brought the proceedings to a halt. She wasn't a bad ventriloquist. With a little better material she could make a living on radio. Sound radio ventriloquists were all the rage and the audiences sitting at home never could see if their lips moved.

Blousey edged closer, nudging the girl in front who was having trouble moving a giant harp. Bugsy helped her on to the middle of the stage with the monumental, gilt-laden instrument. It wasn't really worth it because the very sight of the instrument was enough to put Oscar off.

With the sudden exit of the harp player, Blousey was next, and she tripped rather clumsily on to the stage. Bugsy shouted 'Good luck!' from the wings. Blousey politely announced herself as she handed the pianist her music.

'Er . . . Blousey Brown . . . er, singer.'

She nodded to the pianist to begin the introduction. Blousey opened her mouth to sing—but there was no time for her even to get her first word out, because the inevitable happened. Lena Marrelli returned. You couldn't mistake her or her mink coat and red ringlets, which bounced up and down as she stormed down the centre aisle. Oscar De Velt made no attempt to look displeased at her entrance. A morning going through what he'd been through made it easier to welcome Lena back with open arms—and Oscar's arms were held very, very wide.

51

'Lena, honey, you came back to me.'

Lena screwed up her horrid little precocious face. The freckles on her nose disappeared into the wrinkles that were formed. 'I'll give you one more chance, you hear me, Oscar, otherwise I'm out for good. Out, out, Out!'

Her entourage, who had followed her in, fussed round her as she poked her bony little finger at Oscar. His assistant poked out her tongue behind her clipboard by way of defiance. Oscar repeated himself.

'Lena, honey, you came back to me.'

The audition queue looked on in silence, including Blousey, who was still waiting centre stage to begin her song. Oscar broke away from his returned star long enough to send everybody home. The charade was over.

'O.K., everyone, the audition's finished.'

The hopefuls, the would-be's and the might-have-made-it's walked off like dejected mongrels, their tails between their legs. The harp player dragged away her enormous harp, risking serious injury as she yanked it across the stage. Blousey was very dejected and Bugsy put his arm around her to console her.

'Cheer up. There's a million other jobs.'

'Sure, on the sidewalk with a hat to catch the dimes in.'

Bugsy pushed open the double doors that led off the wings and into a narrow brick corridor at the rear of the theatre. 'It's only a matter of time,' he said rather lamely.

Blousey pulled away from him and kicked at a pile of scenery that toppled over on to the floor with a loud crash.

'Cool off, will you,' Bugsy shouted at her.

Blousey was getting very tearful and shouted back, 'Look. I've been walking the streets of New York for six months now, and the only fancy steps I've done so far are avoiding the man who collects the rent.'

'So it takes time to be a movie star. We could come back tomorrow.'

'Come back tomorrow? Come back tomorrow! Come back! That's all I ever hear. My whole life I've been coming back tomorrow.'

Blousey was getting very distraught, and with this last outburst she let fly with another kick that toppled another pile of scenery to the ground. Bugsy was beginning to get angry.

'Knock it off, will you, Blousey? Cool down.'

'I will not cool down. I will not! I will not!'

By now Bugsy had had enough, and unhooked the fire bucket from the wall. He wasn't quite sure of the contents as he threw it. It could have been sand, but it turned out to be water and it drenched Blousey from head to toe. Blousey screamed with rage. She was wet through—and suddenly her anger subsided and she began to sob instead.

'I'm sorry.'

Bugsy put his arm around her once more. 'Don't worry. There's always Fat Sam's place.'

'He won't see me,' she sniffed.

'I'll talk to him?'

'You know him?'

'Know him? We're like that.' Bugsy crossed his fingers to show how close a buddy of Fat Sam's he was.

'You're real good friends?'

'No. It's just that when I talk to him, I cross my fingers that he won't hit me.'

Blousey laughed for the first time and Bugsy took off his coat and put it over her shoulders. They walked down the corridor laughing as Blousey's feet squelched loudly in her soggy wet shoes.

13. DUMB BUMS WE AIN'T

The sleek black sedan squeaked around the corner. Its occupants made it bulge at the seams, and, really, to call it sleek is to flatter it. Fat Sam's gang fell out rather awkwardly.

They were a ragged bunch of individuals who vaguely answered to the term 'hoodlums', but they frightened themselves a lot more than they frightened anyone else.

They sauntered down the street as if they owned it. Now and again they would push the passers-by to one side, but more often than not this would result in disturbing the padding in their suits rather than inconveniencing their victims. Ritzy and Snake-Eyes helped themselves to an orange from a fruit seller's stall. She was busy serving someone else and didn't catch sight of the theft. However, Louis followed suit and, being Louis, was naturally spotted by the fruit seller as his great banana hands wrapped themselves round an orange. She screamed at him in Italian, and hurled cabbages along with her Sicilian abuse.

At that moment, Fat Sam emerged from the back door of his office and climbed up the stone stairs to street level. At the sight of his gang retreating in cowardly disorder from the enraged fruit seller, a torrent of words left his mouth like buckshot. Fat Sam's mouth, when really stretched, would spread from ear to ear, and on a good day with the wind in the right direction his voice would carry for as many as twenty blocks. He was furious.

'You dummies, can I believe my eyes? You bunch of peanut brains, you hear me? Get out of there, we got business to do. Come on, snap it up in here. In, in, in! Don't hang around. Get your legs movin' in this direction.'

He snapped his fingers to punctuate his words, and turned into the doorway. The gang followed, their heads bowed in a combination of fear and shame. And the way Fat Sam pulled open the door to his office, nearly taking it off its hinges, it was mostly fear.

Sam opened a walnut closet and replaced his grey pinstriped jacket with a gold silk dressing gown. Ritzy attempted to help him on with it but Fat Sam scowled and shrugged him off. The rest of the gang sat down rather timidly. Fat Sam tied the belt of his dressing gown tightly round his fat midriff.

'Right. Let's get down to it.'

Snake-Eyes had nervously started to throw his dice on to the baize of Sam's pool table. He swept them up and threw them down monotonously.

'Don't do that, Snake-Eyes. This is thinking time.'

'Sorry, Boss.'

Sam eased his bulky figure into his chair. Knuckles filled the silence with a crack of his knuckles.

'And don't do that, Knuckles. I'm surrounded by a bunch of nervous wrecks.' Sam absent-mindedly toyed with his letter-opener as he spoke, and dug it into the veneer of his desk top. 'Right. Let's get down to it. I'll start at the beginning. We're being outsmarted by that lounge lizard. Right?'

The gang nodded in agreement.

'And we're gonna get back on top. Right?'

'Right back on top, Boss.'

'We're gonna kick that drugstore cowboy into line. Right?'

'You bet, Boss.'

The gang were certainly not going to disagree with Sam in this mood. They threw nervous glances at one another to make sure they never missed their cues. Fat Sam continued, this time, remarkably, his voice held a trace of humility.

'Sure we've been a little slow off the mark, but dumb bums we ain't.'

'No. Dumb bums we ain't.' The hoods looked at one another as they confidently echoed Sam's words.

They could have fooled no one. A bigger bunch of dumb bums had probably never graced a hoodlum's office than the knuckle-headed crew that sat before Sam. He took them all by surprise as he suddenly changed the subject.

'O.K., Louis. Stand against the wall.'

'Who? Me, Boss?'

'Sure. You, Louis. How many other guys called Louis in this room?'

Louis stood up from the wicker-backed twin-seat that he usually sat in. The wickerwork had sagged a little over the years and Louis's plump bottom fitted very comfortably into the dip. He edged up against the creamy brown wall and jostled the boxing pictures with his elbow. The rest of the gang looked at one another. They were as mystified as Louis. Fat Sam slowly pulled himself out of his chair.

'Ritzy, hand me a pie.'

A pie? thought Louis. Snake-Eyes threw a glance to Angelo, who tugged at his starched collar and gulped awkwardly. A pie? Ritzy got up from his chair and went across to the veneered drinks cupboard. He snapped up the top and took out a silver tray. Six very healthy cream pies sat in two neat rows across it. Sam scooped his podgy hand under one of them and made towards Louis, who sweated at the thought of what might happen.

'What did I do, Boss? Boss? Talk to me, Boss. Tell me what did I do wrong?'

'You didn't do nothing, Louis. Nothing.'

Before Sam had finished his words he had let the pie go. It curved through the air in an expert arc, but Louis was thinking quicker than he'd thought for a long time. His brain told him to duck and he willed his legs to bend at the knees. He ducked just in time. The pie splurged against the wall with a wet 'schplattt', covering the boxing pictures like a sudden fall of snow. Sam strutted back to his desk.

'See what I mean? Missed. O.K., Louis, you can sit down now.'

Louis stood up and, more than a little relieved, eased his bottom once more into the dip in the basket chair.

'Even a dumb mug like Louis is too quick for us. That's the root of our trouble. We're behind the times.'

Knuckles wrinkled his nose and narrowed his eyes. He wasn't really following Sam's line of thought.

'I don't get it, Boss.'

'Knuckles, we're never gonna get on top with this kind of hardware.' He prodded the fluffy cream pies with a stubby forefinger. 'It's old fashioned. In short . . .' Sam paused and looked at his gang, who sat up, waiting for the next piece of wisdom to drop from his lips. '. . . In short, we gotta get ourselves that gun.'

There was silence in Fat Sam's office. If the gang had had any brains, and if brains could clank and whirr like pieces of machinery, the noise would have been deafening. However, the only muffled sound came from Snake-Eyes, as he clicked his dice together in the secrecy of his side pocket.

Suddenly a telephone bell cut through the emptiness left by Sam's remarks. It, too, was muffled, and it was difficult to ascertain where the sound came from. Sure, there was a stick phone on Sam's desk, but that stood silent. Sam bent down and tugged at the handle of the

56

bottom drawer on the far side. As he opened the drawer, the bell sounded clearer as he revealed his secret phone. He snatched at the receiver and stuffed it into the gap between his shoulder and ear.

'O.K. Yeah. Start gabbin'. Yeah, yeah, O.K. Right. You sure now? Right. Thanks. 'Bye.'

The gang strained their ears to hear what was being said. The muffled voice at the other end of the line sounded rather frightened and talked very quickly, making it impossible to follow the conversation. Sam put the receiver back into the cradle and swung his chair round on its squeaky swivel. He tapped the end of his fingers together and smiled. The gang were very relieved. He didn't smile often, and they were grateful if a little sunshine ever drifted their way past his yellow teeth. He leaned back on his chair.

'O.K., you guys. We've had ourselves a little break. Who knows the Hung Fu Shin Laundry Company?'

Ritzy raised a finger. 'Me, Boss.'

'Right. 'Cause my friend on the telephone tells me that's where they stash the guns. Get movin'.'

The gang jumped out of their chairs and made for the door. They didn't need telling twice.

'Not you, Knuckles. I need you here with me.'

Knuckles stopped in his tracks and closed the door after the hoods, who were already on their way to the chinese laundry. He automatically cracked the bones in his fingers and his boss ignored it for once. Sam was already sensing victory. He smiled to himself as he clasped his hands tight across his ample stomach. His fat lips slid into a satisfied smile. But it was a smile that wouldn't be there for long.

14. AL IS IS GIT. OR NOT SO GIT

The Chinese workers mumbled away to one another as they scrubbed at the laundry. Their hands were red and steaming as they yanked the clothes to and fro in the boiling water. A little girl sorted the laundry sacks into piles whilst another was nearly swallowed up by the contents of an enormous laundry basket. There were dozens of these baskets, and neatly painted on the sides of each was *'The Hung Fu Shin Laundry Company'*.

The little girl sorting the bags stiffened as she saw Ritzy come through the door. The rest of Fat Sam's gang followed. They pushed their way past the Chinese workers, who scuttled for cover. Angelo tossed a scrubbing brush into one of the zinc laundry troughs and the hot sudsy water splashed up the front of one Chinaman who hadn't run away. He promptly did so. Snake-Eyes and Ritzy pulled down clothes from the line that was strung across the laundry. Louis, who monotonously shot out his cuffs in his normal impersonation of the legendary Shakedown Louis, trampled on the clothes with his sizeable two-tone boots.

The gang made for the door at the far end of the laundry. It was a solid panelled door, and Ritzy hurt his knuckles as he rapped on it. (Naturally, he was too cool to let on that it hurt.) The rest of the gang sat around in a rather sloppy fashion, not really paying a lot of attention. A bunch of frightened Chinese laundrymen weren't going to give them any trouble. The errand that Fat Sam had sent them on was a piece of cake, they thought. As usual, they thought wrong.

As they waited for the door to open, the lids of four of the huge laundry baskets were suddenly thrown open, and out jumped Bronx Charlie, Yonkers, Shoulders and Benny Lee. Fat Sam's gang spun round in total surprise. One minute they had been nonchalantly chewing at their toothpicks and the next they were staring down the barrels of four nasty-looking splurge guns. They didn't look for long.

Shoulders was the first to pump his trigger, as he let go a salvo of splurge splattered the shiny green tiles above Angelo's head. Suddenly it was raining splurge. The four guns spat out their white, foamy contents around the ears of Fat Sam's four trapped gangsters, who vainly tried to cover behind the piles of washing they had trampled on. The splurge guns never let up, and Benny Lee's face grimaced in time with his trigger finger.

The gang turned white as their various pathetic figures were swamped by the deluge of splurge. One by one they got it. Louis was first. Full in the face, it took his hat off. Snake-Eyes' black face changed colour as the white splurge hit, and moulded itself to the shape of his nose and cheeks. Angelo got his so hard it nearly knocked him into the middle of next week. Ritzy blinked when his come-uppance came—it was just as well. The splurge splattered across his eyes and forced its way up his nostrils. He looked like a cream doughnut in spats.

From the other side of the laundry, Dandy Dan watched the proceedings with delight. He was on top now. Without a gang to aid him, Fat Sam was as helpless as a tortoise without its shell. He took a large bite out of the green apple he was holding and smiled at the sight before him. Up to now he had been ahead on points. Now he knew it wouldn't be long before Fat Sam threw in the towel. The apple tasted good.

The phone in Sam's drawer let out its muffled ring. Sam's podgy hand snatched it up.

'Hello. Yeah. Start gabbin'.'

Sam's bottom jaw dropped six inches as the voice on the telephone told him the bad news. His mouth was still open as he put the phone down. Knuckles knew something was wrong and slid off the side of the pool table where he had been perching. He said nothing— just stared at Sam's white face. It was an eerie sight to see Fat Sam's mouth open so wide and not have your eardrums popping with the noise of his giant vibrating tonsils. Knuckles plucked up enough courage to break the silence.

'Boss?'

'The whole gang's gone, Knuckles. Splurged. That leaves just you and me.'

Knuckles, without thinking, took off his hat to show his respect. He felt a little embarrassment and a lot of loneliness. He looked around at the empty chairs that had once been filled by the gang. As Shakespeare once said, 'When the chips are down, even dumb bums have got a heart'. Knuckles lived up to his name once again and squeezed his fat fingers, letting off a machine gun burst of bone-clicking. Fat Sam threw his note pad at him in disgust.

'Don't do that, Knuckles. How many times do I have to tell you? It irritates me. We do nothing. We act like nothing's happened. Carry on as normal. Tutto casa sono buono.'

The Italian tripped off Sam's tongue. It always did when he was upset. Knuckles looked puzzled.

'What does that mean, Boss?'

Sam stopped biting his nails for a moment to look up at his henchman. 'You don't speak Italian?'

'No, Boss, I'm Jewish.'

Sam translated for him. 'We act like . . . like everything's hunky dory.'

Knuckles nodded and mumbled his own yiddish translation to himself. 'Oh, al is is git.'

But everything wasn't so *git*. And they both knew it.

15. YOU'RE ACES, BUGSY

Fizzy pounded the piano keys with great gusto. The music didn't make sense but he obviously enjoyed it. To outside ears it sounded like a jumble of discords, but in Fizzy's head it sounded beautiful. Whenever he was alone in the speakeasy he would tinkle away at the ivories. Not that he was entirely alone. Jelly, the fat boy who looked after the speakeasy door, was generally his audience. He was tone deaf as well, and would lean over the top of the stairs, his head on his hands, and watch Fizzy with glazed eyes. Unbelievably, considering all that note-thumping, Jelly seemed to be nodding off to sleep. Then Fizzy's tune was interrupted, as Jelly woke up to slide open the speakeasy door and let Bugsy in.

'Hey, Bugsy,' welcomed Fizzy.

'Hey, Fizzy. How you doing?'

'Fine, Bugsy. Just fine.'

'Still practising?'

'Sure thing, Bugsy. Still practising.'

At that moment, Tallulah glided through the door of the girls' room. She leaned over the banister rail and smiled down at Fizzy and Bugsy.

'Suddenly everybody wants to be in show business.'

'Oh, hi, Tallulah. I've come to see Fat Sam. Is he in?'

Tallulah was joined by Tillie, Loretta and Dotty, who slouched over the rail and threw nods and red-lipped smiles in Bugsy's direction. Tallulah didn't like that much. That was her department.

'He's busy, Bugsy. Why don't you have a drink while you're waiting?'

'Why not? I'll have a special on the rocks.'

Tallulah tiptoed down the steep stairs with as much elegance as her high-heeled shoes would allow. Tillie, Loretta and Dotty followed suit. But not for long, Tallulah turned at the bottom and coolly put them into reverse.

'O.K., girls. Go feed the ducks.'

'Oh, Tallulah!' the girls offered as a feeble response, but Tallulah would have none of it.

The girls turned around and clomped noisily back up the stairs. Tallulah smoothed down her skirt and snapped her fingers at the barman, who knew better than to ignore her. He threw ice into two glasses and poured in the bright green 'special' drink that was a favourite amongst the speakeasy's regulars. Bugsy took an up-turned chair from on top of a table and sat himself down. Tallulah pulled a chair across from another table and edged up close to him. She meant business.

Bugsy was not sure he knew how to cope. Up on stage, Fizzy continued his strange 'music'—though it was scarcely romantic. Upstairs, Jelly had finally nodded off to sleep and was snoring quietly. Tallulah put her hand on Bugsy's shoulder and began her attack.

'Long time no see, Bugsy.'

'Well, you know how it is.'

'You used to come and see me every night.'

Bugsy fiddled with his hat brim. 'I've been busy,' he squeaked.

'Busy doing what?'

Tallulah was returning his service with great ease.

'Oh, this and that.'

Bugsy's answers weren't getting any better. Tallulah edged even closer towards him. Fizzy's piano playing had reached a crescendo and Tallulah snapped at him.

'Fizzy, will you quit the ivories and hit the shoe leather.'

'Yes, ma'am.'

Fizzy finished his 'piece' in defiance and then sheepishly closed the lid of the piano. He skulked off, a little moody and upset at being so unceremoniously evicted. The 'specials' arrived and were set down in front of Bugsy and Tallulah. She crisply gave the barman his marching orders.

'O.K. Beat it. Go check the storeroom.'

'Sure thing, ma'am.'

Fat Sam's girl knew who she was and wasn't about to let people forget it. She turned back to Bugsy. This time she was pulling all the stops out.

'You're aces. You know that, Bugsy? I've always found you kind of special.'

'Careful, Tallulah, you're racing my motor.'

He meant what he said. And so did she.

'Come on, Bugsy. Give a girl a break, won't you?'

'You sure you got the right fella?'

Tallulah sighed. 'You're not like those other saps.'

'No?'

'You've got lovely brown eyes. You know that?'

She was inches from him, and she ran a finger along his dark brown eyebrows as she spoke. Bugsy offered a lame joke.

'They'll be lovely black eyes if Fat Sam catches us.'

'How about smearin' my lipstick?'

Tallulah tilted her head on one side and narrowed her eyes at him. She pouted her lips and let out another sigh. Bugsy gulped.

'If you come any closer, I'll call my lawyer.'

Tallulah was not put off. She'd also caught sight of Blousey coming in at the speakeasy door.

'So call him.'

Tallulah leaned across and kissed Bugsy on the forehead. The bright red lipstick made an indelible shape on his swarthy skin. Blousey was dumbstruck. She stormed down the stairs with a loud clatter and Bugsy immediately pulled away from Tallulah.

'Oh, hi, Blousey,' he stammered.

Tallulah sat back in her chair and breathed coolly on her shiny red fingernails. Blousey stormed up the stairs towards Fat Sam's office, ignoring Bugsy's calls after her. She burst through the double doors that led to Fat Sam's inner office. Her knuckles rapped violently on the dappled glass marked 'S. Stacetto Private'. She bit her lip while she waited, more in frustration than in anger. Knuckles answered the door and sighed a bored sigh at seeing her standing there. He didn't bother to ask her what she wanted.

'It's the broad about the audition, Boss.'

Without waiting for a reply from Sam, he took it upon himself to send her away. 'He's busy, lady. Come back tomorrow.'

Blousey's face dropped. She could handle Bugsy and Tallulah, but not getting an audition poleaxed her, and the last drop of courage drained from her face and tears welled up in her eyes. Suddenly Sam appeared at the door, and surprised them both.

'O.K., lady, I'm all ears. Go right in and get ready. We'll be right with you. Just a couple of things to tie up here, and we'll be in there a-listening.'

He smiled a big Italian smile that seemed to be reflected in his shiny, greased-down hair. Blousey, delighted, grabbed her bag and hurtled in the direction of the stage. Sam closed the door and tugged at Knuckles' lapels to bring him down to his own level. Knuckles listened intently. Things were going a little too quickly for him.

Sam whispered as softly as his giant larynx would allow. 'We act as if nothing's happened. Right? We carry on as normal. Right? Like everything's hunky dory. That way they won't know we're scared.' Fat Sam quickly corrected himself. 'I mean concerned.' He couldn't even let Knuckles know how wobbly his knees were getting, as the situation worsened. He patted him on the lapel. 'O.K., Knuckles. Let's go and give this broad a listen.'

Blousey picked up a bentwood chair and moved it to the centre of the stage. Razamataz had sorted out her music and started the piano introduction. He played it like all natural piano players, as if he'd been fingering out that tune every night, six nights a week. In fact, he'd never heard it before.

Sam, Knuckles, and a few of the girls made themselves comfortable, draped over the handrail at the top of the stairs. Bugsy sat down next to Tallulah and sipped his drink nervously, hoping that the previous incident had been forgotten. Fizzy stopped mopping the floor and leaned heavily on his broom. 'At least someone gets an interview around here,' might have been the thought going through his head. But it wasn't. He was enjoying Razamataz's piano-playing too much.

Blousey began to sing, and to the audience's surprise she was rather good. Bangles and Loretta were more difficult to impress. Whenever Tallulah got sick they would stand in for her, and if Blousey got a job they wouldn't get a look in from now on. Blousey looked rather pointedly towards Bugsy during her song. He scratched his forehead in embarrassment and saw the tell-tale lipstick on his fingers. Grabbing his handkerchief, he rubbed away at the evidence. Tallulah threw a worldly glance at the proceedings and smiled to herself. She couldn't understand the fuss.

Sam brought the audition to an abrupt end by clapping his podgy hands together. Blousey was only half way through her song and she feared the worst.

'O.K., honey, that's enough. Very nice. A little contemporary for my tastes, but all the same, very nice. You're hired.' He snapped his fingers for his entourage to follow him back into his office.

Blousey finished the last note of her song, but she'd already lost half her audience. Bugsy applauded nervously as she collected her things together for a speedy exit.

'Great, Blousey. That was really swell. I told you you'd make it. That was terrific, really terrific.'

He might as well have saved his breath. Blousey com-

xy Robinson—splurged!

"Call yourselves hoodlums?"

Dandy Dan's gang burst into the Grand Slam...

"Don't worry, I'll think of something."

"You goofed, Doodle..."

The end of the road for Dan's men...

Blousey Brown

Leroy Smith

Fat Sam Stacetto, with (l. to r.) Louis Knuckles, Snake-Eyes, Angelo and Ritzy

Captain Smolsky and Lieutenant O'Dreary

Fizzy

Babyface

Tallulah

Dan's gang: (l. to r.) Benny Lee, Shoulders, Bronx Charlie, Yonkers, Laughing Boy and Doodle

Bugsy Malone

Dandy Dan

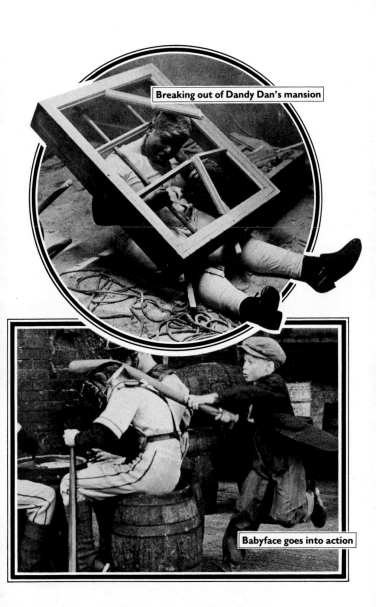

Breaking out of Dandy Dan's mansion

Babyface goes into action

...pies flew in all directions...

pletely ignored him and stormed up the stairs towards
the speakeasy exit. Bugsy called after her.

'Blousey! Blousey!'

The only answer he got was the door crunching closed
as she yanked at the lever that operated the mechanism
in the bookshop front. Bugsy stood up and put his
hat on. Moving away from the table, he corrected himself long enough to hurry back and plant a kiss with
his finger on Tallulah's powdered nose.

'So long, Tallulah. Maybe another time.'

Tallulah twirled the glass in her hand until the cherry
on top of the green liquid got dizzy and drowned. She
scooped it out with her red-nailed fingers and popped
it into her rosebud mouth.

'Sure, sap. I'll believe it when I see it.'

She crunched at the cherry with great venom—and then
spat it out in rather an unladylike fashion. She'd forgotten
that she hated cherries.

Out in the street, Blousey hurried along the sidewalk and
hid behind some barrels that had been dumped outside the Ponti Olive Oil Import Company. Bugsy made
the door of the bookshop just late enough to miss her
and early enough to think he hadn't. He looked hurriedly right and left through the people that hustled
along the busy sidewalk. He ran straight past the Olive
Oil barrels that Blousey was hiding behind and was soon
lost in the crowd. Blousey watched him go, and then
made off in the opposite direction. Bugsy reached the end
of the street and threw down his hat in frustration. He
picked it up and angrily brushed the dust from the brim.
He'd lost her. He hoped it was only for the time
being.

16. LOONEY (OFF HIS TROLLEY) BERGONZI

Razamataz pounded into the black and white ivory keys with the confidence you'd expect from someone who had been playing a piano since he was three years old. In those days, you could have picked up a secondhand mahogany upright for less than twenty dollars, and even in the poorest home it was almost the first purchase after a stove and a kitchen table. There were fourteen children in Razamataz's family, and he had got lucky by being number five. Lucky, that is, because it was the odd numbers that Razamataz's father had decided could learn the piano. The lady who lived upstairs was the local church organist, and for an all-in economy fee of a dollar fifty she would sit patiently with children one, three, five, seven, and so on, and teach them the secrets of the magical sounds that came from those felt hammers pounding the taut metal strings.

The lady who played the organ didn't quite have Fat Sam's speakeasy in mind when she struggled with Razamataz, her favourite pupil. He nodded to the saxophone player to stand up and take his solo, and the spotlight moved off Razamataz to seek out the spotty sax player with ears like taxi-cab doors. Down amongst the appreciative audience, Knuckles struggled with a long tray of six drinks. The green liquid slopped on the round metal tray as he tried to sidestep the customers in the busy speakeasy. He nodded a few hello's to the regulars and smiled with a fixed smile that could have been tied on behind his ears.

In the corridor outside Fat Sam's office, Fizzy jumped up from reading his movie magazine (or more correctly looking at the pictures) when Knuckles backed through the swing doors with his tray of drinks. Through the glass panels that formed one side of Sam's office could be seen the ominous black shapes of his gang. Knuckles opened the door with his free left hand while balancing the tray expertly with his right. Fat Sam sat slouched in his leather chair, nervously clicking two pool balls together in an almost maniac way. He lifted his top lip from his discoloured front teeth in an up and down motion that resembled a shop window blind, revealing the yellow contents of his mouth. Knuckles eyed the wooden cutout figures that lined the wall, throwing the shadows of the gang on to the patterned glass. It was Fat Sam's way of pretending that his gang were still around. Act as normal, he'd said. And that meant letting the world know he was still surrounded by his burly, if incompetent, henchmen. Knuckles interrupted Sam's ball-clicking.

'Show's going swell, Boss.'

He put the tray of drinks down on the veneered drinks cupboard. Sam made him take enormous pains to ask for six green specials at the bar. 'Ask in your loudest voice,' he'd said, and Knuckles had struggled across the floor in a showy balancing display. Life flickered into Sam's staring eyes for the first time.

'Good. We mustn't let 'em know we're beat. We've got to give the impression that we're still on top. That way we can have time to think. Time to breath. Right, Knuckles. Come over here.'

Fat Sam stood up and moved to the boxing picture that sat neatly on the wall behind his head. He clicked a hidden button at the side and the picture sprang forward on secret hinges, revealing a wall safe. Sam stood on a box to reach the dial at the safe's centre. He clicked away confidently. He knew the safe's combination of eight digits off by heart.

'I've sent for someone to help us out of our little predicament. No ten cent dummy. A specialist.'

Knuckles wrinkled his nose up near his eye. He wasn't following Fat Sam's drift.

'A doctor, Boss?'

Sam clicked open the safe and reached deep into the interior. He took out a single photograph about six inches by four in size.

'Not a doctor, you bilberry,' he snapped. 'A hoodlum.'

Knuckles was still puzzled. 'I thought *we* was hoodlums, Boss?'

'Not a dumb bum, Knuckles. This guy's the real McCoy.'

Sam thrust the photograph into Knuckles' hand, and the obedient henchman carefully turned it over to see who it was. As the information reached his brain, his mouth dropped open.

'Not Looney Bergonzi? *The* Looney Bergonzi?'

Fat Sam tapped the photograph with a smug gesture. 'The very same, Looney "Off His Trolley", "Mad as a Hatter", Bergonzi. The best man in Chicago. Right. Here's what we do.'

He snatched the photograph from Knuckles and threw it back into the safe, spinning the dial in one fluid movement. 'We arrange ourselves a meeting with Dandy Dan. Bergonzi will be in the back of the car, next to me. Knuckles, you'll drive.'

'Right,' Knuckles replied quickly, and was half way to the door before he remembered one vital factor. 'But I don't drive, Boss.'

Fat Sam closed his eyes in dismay. 'You don't drive? You great dumb salami. Right. We'll get ourselves a driver.'

Out in the corridor, the girls chatted and giggled as they made their way back and forth between the girls' room and the stage. Bugsy wove his way through them, smiling as he went—probably to hide the embarrassment of the large bunch of flowers he was holding. He rapped on the door of the girls' room and plump Bangles answered it almost immediately.

'Hi, Bangles. Is Blousey there?'

Bangles blew a bubble with her gum as she answered. 'She won't see you, Bugsy.'

He changed hands with the flowers and leaned heavily on the door post. He wasn't being fobbed off that easily.

'Look. Tell her I'm sick, will yuh?'

'You're sick?'

'Yeah. Sick of waiting.'

Bangles blew him a bubble in response to that, and padded off in her Japanese slippers to pass on the message. Bugsy looked at the fifty cent blooms in his hand, and already they seemed to be wilting in the smoky atmosphere. At last Blousey came to the door. She wasn't slow in getting off the mark.

68

'Beat it, wisie.'

'Give a guy a break, will you, Blousey? I brought you some flowers.'

Blousey took them. 'I'll see that Tallulah gets them.'

'Quit being so smart, will you? They're for you.'

At that moment, Fizzy put his arms around Bugsy for balance as he poked his head round the door.

'Five minutes to go.'

Blousey turned away. 'I'll have to go. I'm on stage in five minutes.'

'I'll see you afterwards.'

'Maybe.'

'I was thinking of getting a job.'

Blousey let out a bored sigh as she replied sarcastically, 'You don't get paid for standing in breadlines, buster.'

Bugsy wasn't giving up. 'A legit job, I tell you. We'll save some money—enough for tickets to the coast and Hollywood. Who knows, they're always looking for new movie stars, we could . . .'

But Blousey had had enough. She paused long enough to hand him back the flowers. 'Sure, sure. I'll believe it when I see it. 'Bye.'

The door slammed in Bugsy's face and he kicked his heel against the wall angrily. He looked down at the flowers, which were wilting even more pathetically than before. Fat Sam's interruption caught him off guard.

'Hey, Bugsy. You drive?'

Bugsy looked up in surprise at the fat gangster, who was standing in the doorway to his office. Knuckles peered from behind.

'Sure. Why?'

'How'd you like to earn yourself some green stuff?'

'As long as you're not talking about cabbages, sure.'

Fat Sam beamed all over his face. 'Step inside. I've got a little proposition to make to you.'

Bugsy walked into Fat Sam's office and Sam noticed the flowers. He beamed even wider. 'For me? How nice.' He snatched at the flowers and slapped them into Knuckles' face. 'Knuckles, put these in water. What a nice thought. Bugsy, yous and me are gonna get on just fine.'

Knuckles closed the door behind them, spitting the flower petals out of his mouth.

17. THE SALAMI

Smolsky and O'Dreary burst through the double swing doors into the Hung Fu Shin Chinese laundry. The steam from the hot water troughs had subsided and there was washing strewn all over the floor. The two cops stayed long enough to take in the empty scene. The place was deserted. Smolsky deduced that wherever the Chinese laundry workers and Dandy Dan's gang were, it wasn't here. The two City Hall bloodhounds turned on their heels and scampered out as quickly as they had come in.

The phone rang in Dandy Dan's living room—rather spoiling the efforts of the smartly-dressed string quartet which bravely struggled through the piece that Dan had insisted they play. In fact, to give him his due, he had been a little more general. 'Play it classical, and play it loud', had been his instructions. He really didn't know how bad they were.

A hairdresser clipped away at Dandy Dan's already immaculate head, and teeny slithers of hair floated down like butterfly wings on to the white cloth covering his shoulders. Louella, Dan's blonde, polo-playing companion —as immaculate as he was—sat in a soft, pink satin dressing gown with mink cuffs. She struggled with an enormous jigsaw that she had seen someone do in a movie. She wasn't having a great deal of success, as she had only managed to join a few pieces of sky together to form a rather ragged top line. It wasn't much, but it was a start. She had never claimed to be a genius. When you look as beautiful as she did, nature has a way of making you dumb to redress the balance with the rest of us mortals.

Dan's ears might not have told him that his lead violinist was off key—but they did tell him that the phone call his butler had just answered was important.

'You're wanted on the telephone, sir,' murmured Johnson. 'A Mr Fat Sam Stacetto.'

Dan got up immediately and walked over to his chromium-plated personal phone. He threw off the white barber's cloth and revealed a snazzy, neatly-pressed, silver brocade dressing gown. He smoothed down the white silk lapels as he picked up the receiver.

'Hello. This is Dandy Dan speaking.'

In Sam's office, the red Coca Cola sign in the street outside bled its coloured light across the wall and on to Sam's face.

'I want to meet you, Dan, to do a little talking.'

'Where?'

'East Chester Park. Fiveways, by the crossroads at Lexburg and Denver. You hearing me?'

'Yeah, I'm hearing you, Sam. No hoods, mind.'

'No hoods. You have my word. Monday, eleven a.m.'

'Just you and a driver.'

'Agreed.'

Dan put down the chromium phone and smoothed his moustache with his forefinger.

'Got him. The knucklehead.'

Sam swivelled in his chair and his huge head blotted out the red Coke sign that breathed in and out behind him. He was pleased.

'Got him, The salami. O.K., Knuckles, let's go and enjoy the show.'

On stage, Tallulah edged out from amongst the rest of the girls, who moved as smoothly as if they were made of marshmallow. Tallulah walked down the stairs and the spotlight picked her out as she wove in and out of the customers, teasing and tantalising them with her slinky singing. She knew how to hold an audience, and the chorus girls, moving in contorted, rhythmic circles on the stage, seemed to give a faint glow that evaporated in the air compared with the lasting, lingering magic that flowed from Tallulah, and engulfed everyone.

18. THE CHASE

The birds were whistling at eleven a.m. on Monday morning at the junction of Fiveways at Lexburg and Denver. They obviously didn't know what Fat Sam had on the agenda.

Bugsy shielded his eyes from the sun with his hand as he scoured the five roads that led to the Fiveways intersection. So far, there was no sign of anyone. Bugsy checked his wristwatch, which said three minutes after eleven. Dan was late.

Bugsy leaned on the side of Fat Sam's black sedan and drummed on the roof with his fingers. Inside, sitting in the back seat, were Sam and Looney Bergonzi, who was holding two pies in his hands. Not ordinary pies, but light green fluffy specials that would see off the toughest gangster. Looney had a face that was well named. His glassy staring eyes, wide open, were fixed, unblinking, in their sockets. Sam gave him a pat on the cheek with the back of his hand but Looney offered no response. Sam shrugged his Italian shoulders—there seemed no flickering of human life at all in Looney's mad gaze.

Suddenly, Bugsy banged on the roof of the sedan and Sam jumped in alarm.

'They're coming!'

Jackson, Dandy Dan's chauffeur, was stylishly peddling Dan's immaculate bike sedan down the avenue of tall pines.

Fat Sam pushed Looney under the back seat. 'O.K., Looney. Get out of sight. Keep your head down. You know what to do. Wait until I give you the O.K. Right?'

Looney said nothing. He held the fluffy green pies in the palms of his hands, ready for the act that had made him famous.

Jackson pulled on the hand brake at the side of his sedan and came to a squeaky halt in the soft mud. Dan opened his door and climbed out at the same time as

Sam. The two hoods didn't take their eyes off one another as they straightened their coats. Sam's jacket, always too small for him, had crumpled up into a concertina during the journey to Fiveways. Dan, of course, looked like he'd walked straight out of his tailor's fitting room. He coughed elegantly into his cupped hand and was the first to speak.

'What can I do for you, Sam?'

'How about a small dose of straight talk, Dan?'

Dan smoothed his moustache with his forefinger. 'Suits me.'

'You've been taking liberties, Dan.'

'I've been taking what's mine.'

'Trouble is, it belongs to me.'

'Too bad.'

Neither of them was going to give an inch. It was obvious to Sam he wasn't getting anywhere by being tough, so he tried a different tack—being humble. It didn't come easy.

'Now, I'm sure we can talk things over sensibly, Dan. We've been in this game a long time, yous and me. After all, I'm a businessman!'

'You're a dime-a-dozen gangster, Sam.'

This remark hit Fat Sam deep in the gut. He responded in the only way he knew how, and started shouting at the dapper figure.

'Now, you button your lip, mister. Don't talk dirty to me. I don't like your mouth. I have to have some respect.'

'You'd slit your own throat for two bits plus tax.'

The blood ran up into Sam's head and his bulbous cheeks puffed out like big red apples. 'You keep your wisecracks behind your teeth, mister.'

'Keep talking,' smirked Dan.

Sam regained his cool with an effort and tugged at the bottom of his jacket. The creases pulled out for a moment but soon bounced back when he let go.

'I have my position to think of,' he said in a pompous tone.

Dan knew he had Sam by the throat and, like a well-trained bulldog, he wouldn't let go. 'Right now, it's not worth a plug nickel.'

'You're a dirty rat, Dan.'

'You've been watching too many movies, Sam.'

Sam wasn't going to listen to any more. He'd had

enough of straight talk and now he was going to bend it a little.

'O.K., Looney. Let him have it!'

As Looney jumped up from his secret position in the back of the car, Dan yelled, 'Yonkers! Charlie! It's a double-cross!'

Dandy Dan wasn't playing it straight either—and out of the woods jumped Yonkers, Bronx Charlie, Shoulders and Benny Lee. Sam's eyes nearly popped out of his head—and his jaw dropped when he saw that they were all carrying shiny new splurge guns. Looney seemed as over-awed by the presence of the guns as Sam, who croaked, 'Come on, Looney. Let 'em go.'

'O.K., yous guys—freeze.'

Looney's deep monotone dribbled into nothingness. It was like shouting 'Halt!' to a runaway locomotive bearing down on you at fifty miles an hour. The hoods' splurge guns burst into action and gave Looney his answer. It couldn't have been more than fifteen seconds before Looney Bergonzi was on the receiving end of a gallon or two of splurge that splattered on and about him until he resembled a winter snowman.

Bugsy's reflexes had been a little quicker than Looney's. He'd ducked down behind the large chrome headlamps for safety, as Sam clawed his way back into the bike sedan. The splurge pellets splattered around the fat gangster, and as he pulled the door closed, his hat was knocked off by a white missile and plastered against the back of the sedan. Bugsy called to Looney, but his shouts fell on deaf ears. Looney 'Off His Trolley, Mad as a Hatter' Bergonzi was well out of the game. Whatever game that was.

Bugsy thought quickly. The hoods were too busy peppering the side of Sam's car to notice his lightning sprint into the woods at the side of the intersection. And Dan was too busy gloating at Sam's frantic retreat to spot Bugsy creeping through the bushes. Suddenly Bugsy reappeared—and waved his arms. 'Over here, you guys. Over here.'

The hoods, ready for any challenge, ploughed through the greenery after him. Dan couldn't believe his eyes as he saw them vanish down the alleyway of overhanging ferns, for Bugsy had already sidestepped them and was on his way back to the intersection. Dandy Dan bellowed desperately, 'Come back here, you dummies. He's given you the slip!'

Bugsy ran straight at Jackson, and butted him with his head. The chauffeur's shiny leather boots waved in the air as he was upended. Dan took refuge inside his car. Physical contact just wasn't his game, and there was no way he would risk ruining his hundred dollar suit. He pulled down the roller blind—presumably with the logic that to shut your enemies out of sight makes them go away.

He needn't have worried. Bugsy made straight for Fat Sam, who had regained his composure in the back of his bike sedan. He clapped his hands as Bugsy jumped into the driver's seat and pumped hard at the pedals. The solid rubber wheels skidded through the soft gravel and the sedan hit the track at speed. Dan poked his head out of the window of his car and yelled at his gang—who were wandering about in puzzled disarray, looking for Bugsy amongst the overgrown ferns. 'You stupid bunch of salamis! Get back here straight away. They're getting away.'

The gang charged back towards the intersection. By now they were breathing heavily and they panted hard, their wobbly legs bending under the weight of the heavy splurge guns. Shoulders and Bronx Charlie jumped on to the tailboard of Dan's car, and Benny Lee, his round Chinese face grimacing with concentration, jammed himself into the passenger seat. Yonkers leaned heavily against the back of the car and, with a combination of his muscle and Jackson's flashing feet on the pedals, the bike sedan lurched off in pursuit of Sam and Bugsy.

The two sedans wove dangerously in and out of the tall pine trees, jumping high in the air as the solid tyres cracked over uncovered roots. Shoulders and Bronx Charlie tried to fire at the escaping vehicle, but there was no way they could take accurate aim with the car bobbing up and down like a roller-coaster.

Bugsy bit his bottom lip in determination as he steered the bike sedan through the narrow roads that crisscrossed the forest. He turned the steering wheel hard right, and Sam's sedan responded with a two-wheeled skid that nearly upended them. In the back seat, Sam rolled around like a pea in a whistle. From time to time, he would regain his balance long enough to look out of the side window and shake a clenched fist at the following car.

Dandy Dan urged Jackson onwards. The sweat was pouring down the chauffeur's ebony face and he wished he wasn't wearing the tight-collared, thick wool chauffeur's suit that Dan insisted upon. His boots were a blur as they did their best work on the pounding pedals. Bugsy took a brief look round to see that Dandy Dan's snazzy tan sedan was gaining on him. Suddenly Fat Sam let out a yell.

'Bugsy! Look out!'

Bugsy hadn't noticed the slow-moving truck that had pulled straight out across the track. It was heavily laden with the entire family and possessions of some luckless, evicted farmer. The farm children clung to the side, sitting on mattresses tied on tightly to stop them toppling over. Bugsy hauled madly on the wheel. He missed them by a whisker—and ploughed through the narrow ditch at the side of the track. The solid wheels spun in the mud. For a moment, it looked as though they were stuck. Then, suddenly, one wheel bit into the ground and the car took off once more.

Behind them, Dandy Dan's sedan had braked even more heavily, and had spun off the road in a different direction. Jackson was having trouble getting the car out of the soft mud, and Shoulders put his considerable muscle behind the back wheel to lurch the sedan into movement once more. Grinning at his muscular effort, Shoulders jumped nonchalantly on to the running board with a practised cool that had taken years to perfect. He needn't have bothered. He missed the step by a good foot as the sedan surged away, and ended up flat on his face in the mud. Dan waved the incident aside and urged Jackson on without him.

Bugsy had turned down a slight incline and was fairly flying along when he hit the stone that turned him off the road into the chicken shack. There was a terrible sound of crashing and clucking as the car ploughed straight through, to the great consternation of the shack's occupants. Jackson cut the corner after them—but there was no way he could miss the shack, and Dandy Dan was given an equally unwelcome reception by the chickens. As Sam's car careered out of the exit at the far end, the vehicle was hardly recognisable. Covered with straw and infuriated hens, it looked like a mad, mobile haystack. Sam threw a couple of chickens out of his window and they fluttered in the air before coming to rest twenty yards on. They both pecked at the ground, quite unruffled, as if nothing had happened. Dandy Dan's car slowed down a little whilst Dan emptied the back compartment of its feathered lodgers and Jackson pulled the hay from his face—and Bugsy's black car shot ahead.

Fat Sam continued to throw abuse at his pursuers, delighted to see that the tan sedan wasn't quite so snazzy after the chickens had been to work on it. But his jeers didn't slow it down, and despite its heavier load it was closing fast.

Bugsy couldn't help but drive straight through the picnic.

The picnic family quietly sipped their homemade lemonade and nibbled at their hard-boiled eggs. They enjoyed the sunshine and lazed quietly on the grass, watching the occasional fluffy cloud scuttle past above them. It was a peaceful place, they thought, until Bugsy and Jackson whipped over the brow of the hill and turned their picnic spot into a racetrack.

The family dived left and right, out of the path of the two sedans that bulldozed across the tablecloth, through flying plates of salad and sweet pickle. Dan offered a slight apology by tipping his hat to them out of the back window, but he was in no mood to be polite right now. He urged Jackson to pump even harder, but the faithful chauffeur was almost spent and the muscles inside those tight leather boots were beginning to turn to jelly. Benny Lee's expression hadn't changed—he still grimaced with great determination. On the other hand, he might have been a little scared.

Bugsy made a last attempt to throw off his pursuers, and risked toppling Sam's sedan over completely by turning on a dime—and taking a right so sharp you could cut your finger on it. Jackson responded to the challenge, but luck wasn't with him. Suddenly there was a painful yelp of tortured metal as the steering wheel snapped off in his hand. Benny Lee's resolute grimace left his Chinese face for the first time. Dandy Dan shouted in vain, 'Put it back, you fool! Put it back.'

Jackson struggled with the wheel, but it was all over for the Dandy Dan gang. They ploughed through a fence and plummetted over the top of the hill—to land in a lake. The once-snazzy tan sedan hit soft mud with a dull thud—and the hoods were catapulted forwards into the cold muddy water. Dandy Dan stood, waist deep, in the lake. He glimpsed the heavy splurge guns as they sank to the bottom. His soaking gang watched motionless as he threw his crumpled homburg into the water, and combed back his dishevelled hair with his open fingers. He needn't have bothered, because his hair stood on end, leaving a muddy black impression of his hand on his forehead. For a moment—for the first time in his life—he looked a mess. Not so Dandy Dan. And he didn't like it.

Bugsy and Fat Sam were jumping around in their car with joy at Dan's watery mishap. Sam hugged Bugsy so hard he almost cracked his ribs. He also threw out the last of the chickens, which had fallen asleep under his seat.

'Get out of here, you dumb cluck. Go cock-a-doodle-doo somewhere else.'

He took out a wad of money from his side pocket and began peeling off crisp, green, hundred dollar bills. Bugsy watched, mouth open.

'You did very well, Bugsy. I'm very pleased with you. You drove like a madman, you hear me? That makes me very pleased. Here's two hundred dollars for your trouble.'

Bugsy took it. He hadn't seen so much money since that twenty to one winner at the racetrack three seasons back.

'Why, thank you, Mr Stacetto. That's really nice of you. Two hundred dollars. Wow.'

Sam patted him affectionately on the shoulder. Chicken feathers floated up into the air.

'Treat yourself to a new suit. Get rid of that laundry sack you're wearing. Oh, here's the name of my tailor.' He handed Bugsy a visiting card from his front vest pocket. 'Do yourself a favour. Go see him. Get yourself fitted up real fine—real snazzy. Your friends won't know you. And what's more, you don't have to pay for six months.'

'Thank you very much, Mr Stacetto.'

'My pleasure, my boy. Think nothing of it. O.K. Let's get out of here.'

Bugsy let off the brake and the sedan lurched forward once more. Fat Sam eased himself comfortably into the back seat. He brushed a few loose chicken feathers from his face and revealed a huge smile that totally engulfed his features. There was no hiding that he was pleased with himself. He was on top again—for a while, at least.

19. NO ROUGH STUFF

The sign had been put up a long time ago. In big, bold letters it read, *'No Rough Stuff, Fighting, or Spitting in this Dressing Room. By Order of the Management'*. The red ink letters shouted loud—and would have made a lumberjack think twice about breaking a chair over someone's back. Not that a lumberjack would have got past the door of the girls' dressing room, above which the ominous sign hung.

Bangles looked at herself in the large stand-up mirror that had as many costumes draped over it as there were brown stains on its silver surface. She pulled faces at herself to make her dumpy, round face look passably attractive. She twisted and contorted her nose in the air and stretched her neck to try and unfold her tubby double chins. She was jostled by the rest of the girls as she studied her new purple dress.

Obviously, they hadn't noticed. She was sure she looked stunning in it. Well, nearly sure. She had blown two weeks' wages on it and was determined that she looked terrific, no matter what. She coughed loudly to gain the other girls' attention. They were more interested in themselves, as they pampered their porcelain faces and buffed up their glossy red nails. Bangles twisted around once more and the purple chiffon frills fluttered about her.

'What do you think? Don't you think I look cute?'

Tillie interrupted her nail-painting to look at Bangles' puce nightmare of a dress. In all honesty, it was the kind of dress that was left in the store window even when it had been offered at a ridiculously knocked-down price. But Bangles, being Bangles, had gone and bought it. Tillie managed to keep her comments polite.

'I don't know, Bangles. Maybe . . . well . . .'

Bangles wasn't taking a chance on her not liking it and she abruptly turned to Dotty for praise. Dotty was busy making the most of the freckles on her nose. As she spoke, she hardly looked up from her mother-of-pearl hand mirror. 'Er . . . I don't know, Bangles. Perhaps the colour's wrong.'

'What are you talking about?' Bangles snapped. 'Purple's my colour. I always wear purple. Don't I always wear purple?'

'It matches your nose,' Loretta butted in, and Bangles stuck her tongue out at her in reply. Dotty tried to save the situation from slipping into an all-out, hair-pulling, girls' brawl.

'Maybe it's the length.'

'It's the latest length. I read it in the magazine. Here, look.' Bangles snatched at the film magazine Loretta was reading. She didn't bother to ask her if she could borrow it. Bangles and Loretta rarely spoke to one another—apart from their battles of wits and insults. Bangles flicked quickly through the magazine and stabbed at a picture of Lena Marrelli, the fickle star.

Tillie broke in to try and calm the conversation down. 'Maybe it's the frills—they stick out too much, Bangles.'

'It matches her ears!' Loretta added.

Bangles pulled an ugly face at her. 'Frills are in. Look at this picture of Lena Marrelli.'

'Lena Marrelli's not Bangles Dobell,' offered Dotty.

'So what's wrong with Bangles Dobell? You think it'd look any better on you?'

'It'd look better on a horse.' Loretta chirped. By now Bangles had had enough of them. She threw the magazine at Loretta and turned her back on them, trying to be tough, but more than a little hurt inside. She patted her hair as she looked at her face in the mirror, chewing energetically on her gum.

'Can I help it if my looks are ahead of their time?'

'They're what?' the girls replied in unison.

'Full of character, kind of earthy.'

'Yeah. Like a bucket of mud.' Loretta got in the last

insult and smiled rather smugly because it was probably her best.

'You creeps, get lost,' retorted Bangles.

At the other end of the dressing room, Blousey sat staring out of the window. She hadn't heard the argument. She had been too far away in thoughts of her own. The misty glass was in need of a clean and it made the view of the dirty alley at the back of the speakeasy look hazy, almost dreamy. Blousey had been sitting staring for a good twenty minutes. She had been powdering her face with a fluffy red powder puff before thoughts of Hollywood and stardom had taken her by the hand and enticed her into dreamland. Her reverie was interrupted by Bangles, who had stomped across to slump against the wall by the window. She blew a ridiculously large, perfectly formed bubble with her gum. As she gathered it in with her tongue after the bubble had exploded she turned to Blousey.

'What do you think, Blousey? Do you think I look terrible?'

Bangles was working on Blousey's polite nature. Since Blousey had joined the show she had set a sort of record by not shouting at anybody or getting involved in arguments. She had miraculously managed to dodge the insults that rattled around the girls' room. Blousey looked up.

'You tell me, Blousey. Do I look cute, or do I look terrible?'

Blousey looked at Bangles' unfortunate purple dress. There was no way she could have said it looked cute. If the dress had been anything less than a monstrosity she could have got away with, 'It's O.K.', or maybe even 'Not bad', but this was no passable mistake. This was a full-scale chiffon disaster and Blousey had difficulty in lying.

'Honestly?'

It was only one word, but it said all. Bangles' dumpy face dropped, and her double chins folded over one another in a position they were much more at home in. She spoke miserably and honestly to herself. 'Bangles Dobell, you look terrible'. She punctuated her sentence by blowing another large bubble that burst and splattered in a sticky mess across her glossy red lips. She looked back at

Blousey, who had gone back to staring out of the window. 'What are you looking at, anyway?'

'Nothing.'

Blousey didn't look up. Nothing is what she was gazing at, but nothing was certainly not what she saw. The dirty window panes turned the alley into a misty, magic stage that Blousey's mind wandered across. The trash cans were overflowing, filled with garbage that had been carefully given the once-over by the ginger alley cat. Blousey's eyes sparkled as her mind and her hopes conjured up a pretty ballerina, who magically appeared in the alleyway. She danced through the old newspapers and broken grocery boxes as if they weren't there. The light caught the white layers of her ballet dress. The hard sidewalk out front from Mama Lugini's restaurant must have been hard on the ballerina's soft silver ballet shoes as she danced and floated to the gentle music that was nowhere but in Blousey's head. But dreams don't allow such worries.

Flash bulbs burst, and their reflections seemed to sparkle in Blousey's eyes as she thought of Lena Marrelli. That was the kind of star Blousey wanted to be. She thought of the words she had shouted at Bugsy in the Bijoux Theatre. 'I've been walking the streets of New York for six months now and the only fancy steps I've done so far are to avoid the man who collects the rent'. They echoed in her head as she thought of how things might have been. Velma's voice brought her thudding back to reality.

'Blousey, you're wanted on the phone. It's Bugsy.'

Blousey shook the daydreams out of her mind. She made a point of ignoring Tallulah on her way to the phone, but Tallulah managed to get a sly jab in as she went through the door.

'Give him my love.'

Blousey picked up the telephone earpiece.

'Hello.'

Bugsy was talking from a pay booth that had been conveniently situated directly under the elevated railway. He raised his voice as a train clanked, squeaked and thundered past.

'Hello, Blousey. It's Bugsy.'

'Where are you?'

'Oh, around. Listen. I can't talk to you now, but I've just made two hundred bucks.'

Blousey wasn't really in the mood to be impressed—she'd had her fill of fast talk. 'You mean you printed it yourself?'

'No, I earned it,' he protested.

'Doing what?'

'Oh, this and that.' He wasn't giving anything away. Another train pulled away from the station and the lighted coaches threw flickering patterns across his face.

'Who for?' Blousey persisted.

'Fat Sam.'

If Blousey made a good job of hiding the fact that she was impressed, she certainly couldn't keep the surprise out of her voice.

'Fat Sam gave you two hundred dollars?'

'And the loan of his bike sedan for the afternoon.'

'I don't believe you. You're putting me on.'

But she should have believed him, because it was true.

20. KETCHUP WITHOUT

Blousey beamed all over her face as Bugsy wrestled with the steering wheel and Sam's shiny black bike sedan bumped its way along the dusty country roads. Blousey held on to her flapping hat as Bugsy's feet flashed away at the pedals and the vehicle gathered speed.

He drove for as long as it took to escape New York. Streets and buildings of stone and brick gave way to scenery that was a little less man-made. A little more inviting.

At the side of a lake Bugsy discovered a boat, nestling amongst the creepers growing along the bank. With much persistence, he managed to persuade Blousey to join him in the ramshackle, rickety vessel. His attempts at rowing would have won him no medals at the Olympic Games—and soon he was worn out trying. He lay back in the sun, a makeshift fishing line tied around his big toe. Blousey unpinned her hat and closed her eyes to enjoy the warm breeze on her face. Bugsy needn't have bothered to keep an eye on his bobbing cork float because all afternoon he didn't catch a thing. Except, that is, the nice warm smiles that Blousey threw in his direction.

Evening came very quickly—and found them back in town outside Farara's drugstore. Blousey patched up her make-up in the sedan while Bugsy joined the queue for hot dogs. She twirled her hair around her fingers to put back the waves and curls the afternoon wind had blown away.

Bugsy walked back to the sedan with two hot dogs that burned his fingers even though they were wrapped in paper napkins.

'Mustard with onions? Or ketchup without?'

'Ketchup without. What's this?'

Bugsy had placed a brown parcel in her lap. Almost as big as a shoe box, it was wrapped in pink paper and tied with a big bow.

'Who knows? Open it.'

'What is it—a finger bowl?'

'No, wisie, a present.'

Blousey tore at the pink wrapping paper to find a cardboard box. Inside was a small, tortoiseshell nickelodeon viewer. It gleamed under the street lights as she took it out.

'Oh, Bugsy, it's fantastic. Beautiful—really beautiful.'

'Nice?'

'What is it?'

'What is it? It's a viewer, dummy. Look, you turn the handle. All the Hollywood stars.'

Blousey's face lit up as the pictures flicked through. Then her face changed as she put the viewer down again.

'Oh, if only I could get to Hollywood.'

'You can.'

'Sure, I know, wise guy. In the front row of the Roxy Theatre on East 38th Street.'

'No, *really* get to Hollywood.'

'Keep talking.'

Bugsy pushed his hat to the back of his head and counted out aloud on his fingers. 'One eighty for the viewer. Right? Ten cents for the hot dogs. Leaves a hundred and ninety-eight dollars and ten red cents for . . .'

'Surprise me.'

'Two tickets.'

Blousey was still acting wary. 'Two tickets?'

'How many tickets do you need?'

'Two tickets to where? The ball game?'

'Two tickets to Hollywood, dummy!'

Blousey, at last, dropped her cool, and her face lit up. Her stay in New York hadn't exactly been a successful one. She had been fed up for so long that even when she heard good news it took a long time to sink in. But when the good news hit her, it hit her zonk between the eyes—and she threw her arms around Bugsy.

'Oh, Bugsy! That's fantastic, that really is.'

As she grabbed him, his hat tipped up and covered his eyes. He smiled as he tried to pull away from her.

'Knock it off, will you.'

'You're putting me on.'

'It's the honest truth, I tell you.' He crossed his heart and kissed his finger and touched her on the nose. 'But right now I'd better take you home and get Fat Sam's car back, else we won't be going anywhere.'

He stuck his hot dog between his teeth like an extra in a pirate movie and let off the hand brake. The bike sedan lurched forward and Blousey was nearly thrown off her seat. Not that she noticed. She had gone back to her viewer. It had only cost a dollar eighty, but to her it was a dreamland you couldn't put a price to.

21. LEROY SMITH

Bugsy dropped Blousey at her door and stepped on the pedals extra hard to get the bike sedan to Fat Sam's place. It had rained a little, and the shower had left the roads slippery so that he had a job keeping the sedan steady as he took the corners at speed. He'd promised Sam he would leave the car in the alleyway at the side of the Stacetto Brothers' bookstore—the front for Fat Sam's place.

The red tail lights glowed as Bugsy stood on the foot brake and the tyres squealed to a halt on the wet road. At the blind end of the alley was a door with a letter box in the centre. Bugsy strolled towards it. The door was the rear entrance to the speakeasy. Bugsy popped the car keys through the letter box and turned to walk back to the main street. He whistled to himself, more for company than entertainment, because the alleyway was dark and narrow and not the cosiest place to be late at night.

As he turned from the door, he heard a strange sound. He furrowed his brow and cocked his head to one side to listen. There it was again. A sort of low moan. It seemed to come from amongst the garbage and trash cans that adorned the end of the alley. He walked towards the sound, and the moan got louder.

'Is anybody there? Is anybody in there?'

He walked closer, very slowly, and could just make out a dirty-faced figure lying amongst the garbage. He moved in for a better look. Lying there, face down, was a ragged old down-and-out. He was slumped in a desperate position, his arms and legs crumpled underneath him like twisted pipe cleaners. Bugsy played the good Samaritan and tried to pick him up. It was a mistake.

No sooner had he leaned down to help the fellow when he felt a sharp pain—as two heavy hob-nailed boots planted themselves in the middle of his back. Bugsy fell to his knees and the drowsy down-and-out recovered quicker than if he'd taken a dose of Colonel Jacob's patented Milwaukee Pick-Me-Up. Bugsy, dazed, but still with his wits about him, struggled desperately with the two hobos.

If things had stayed that way, he might well have held his own, saved his money and even got a pat on the back from the local precinct police. But things turned out differently, because the two down-and-outs were soon joined by three more, then by six others—until a dozen, dirty-faced, shabbily-dressed hobos were belting into our unfortunate hero.

One of the hobos reached into Bugsy's vest pocket and snatched his earnings from Fat Sam. Bugsy winced from another punch and didn't even feel the precious greenbacks vanish. In fact, things were going so badly for Bugsy that he might have ended up as another piece of garbage on the pile, if it had not been for a large black lad who at that moment was strolling past the alley. He was whistling to himself and pondering what he would be doing for supper with ten cents in his pocket. He'd ruled out the Waldorf Grill—and then he did a double take, as he noticed the fighting amongst the trash cans.

Bugsy, going under for the sixth time, suddenly saw three of the hobos laid into with the crispest left hook he'd ever seen. The black boy's punches flashed right and left so fast they whistled through the air. He tossed the last down-and-out headlong into the alley like a sack of dirty laundry at Hung Fu Shin's. The rest of the hobos ran off into the street—the ones that could still run—side-stepping the passing bike sedans that hooted and swerved.

The boy helped Bugsy to his feet.

'They take your money, mister?'

Bugsy winced as he slapped his pockets. The money had gone. 'Yeah, nearly two hundred dollars.'

The black boy brushed his hat and took off his jacket to clean off the dust. He revealed a pair of yellow webbing braces that held up his baggy trousers. In fact, the trousers were so enormous there was room for three more boys inside, and the braces were so wide that they looked as if they could hold up the Brooklyn Bridge with ease. Bugsy picked up his own hat from the garbage.

'It was nice of you to help me like that.'

'Oh, it was nothing,' replied the chubby-faced boy. As he grinned, his cheeks bulged out like big, shiny, black apples. His teeth sparkled like a toothpaste billboard on the freeway and he smiled with a smile that came easy.

The two of them walked towards the street.

'You must be a boxer. Right?' asked Bugsy.

'Nope,' came the reply.

'You're not? But that's the best punching I ever saw.'

The boy smiled again. His large eyes flashed as his eyelids fluttered with unaffected modesty. Bugsy was curious. He'd come across a lot of boxing talent in his time, but this was the best he'd ever set eyes on.

'You ever been coached?'

'Nope.'

'Ever thought of taking it up?'

'Nope.'

Bugsy persisted. 'Why not? You could be a champion.'

The boy shrugged and smiled once more—a sad smile this time. 'Never had the chance.'

'I know someone who can help you. You know Cagey Joe?'

'Nope.'

'You know Sluggers Gym?'

'Nope.' This time the boy's smile was enormous—it spread from ear to ear and his mouth seemed filled with twice as many teeth as a normal person's.

'What's your name, anyway?'

The boy thought for a while. He was no scholar but his name was something he did know. 'Er . . . Smith. Leroy Smith!'

Bugsy put an arm around his new-found friend and thrust out his hand. 'Put it there, Leroy. You've got yourself a manager.'

The two boys shook hands and Bugsy winced once more. Partly from Leroy's iron grip, and partly from the black and blue reminders of the down-and-outs' boots.

'You know the first thing I'm going to do with you, Leroy?'

Back came Leroy's favourite answer. 'Nope.'

'I'm going to treat you to one heck of a meal.'

'I thought they took your dough, man?'

'Who needs dough?' Bugsy tossed his arms in the air to emphasise his words. He shouldn't have, because it made the ache in his back and the bruises on his ribs seem worse. He gasped again and Leroy put his arm around him for support as they walked off towards the brighter side of town. Away from those dark alleys, Bugsy thought to himself. But he needn't have worried any longer—with Leroy Smith as a partner he could take on the world.

22. GOODBYE KNUCKLES

Captain Smolsky leaned back confidently in the back of the police car. Up front, O'Dreary struggled with the pedals of the bike sedan and the sweat glistened on his forehead from the effort. Smolsky had no reason to look confident—he was about as near to solving this case as O'Dreary was to breaking the world land speed record. But his career hadn't been all failure. He chewed on his pencil as he pondered over his successes. Actually, 'success' would put it more accurately.

It had been the famous 'Black Sox' scandal. The case that had shocked the baseball-going public so deeply in 1919. Smolsky had been on loan to the Californian Police at the time. The New York Commissioner had thought it wise to give the city a rest from the Polish super sleuth (as he was generally referred to in high places). There was also the chance that Smolsky might like the sunshine or the eucalyptus trees and stay there for good. As it turned out, Smolsky surprised everyone, including himself, and had the triumph of his career.

He and a number of other junior detectives had been given instructions to nose around the baseball fraternity to try and weasel out any information they could relating to suspected 'fixed' baseball games. The world series that year was at Red Bluff, between the Chicago White Sox and the Cincinnati Reds. After the best of nine series, the underdog Reds won 5–3. A lot of money had changed hands and the police uncovered the fact that several White Sox players had taken bribes from gamblers to deliberately 'throw' the game. Eight players later testified to a Chicago grand jury admitting that they had deliberately played badly for money. Smolsky had been in on the investigation from the beginning, and he returned from his Californian mission covered in glory. Since then, however, Smolsky's career had been one long climb up the ladder of success in a downwards direction.

But this case was different, he kept telling himself. If he could only repeat his 'Black Sox' success on his own territory, it would wipe his slate clean. And a lifetime of blunders meant a long list, a lot of chalk and a lot of wiping.

The sedan whispered its way through the trees and squeaked to a halt at Dandy Dan and Fat Sam's meeting place—Fiveways, at the intersection of Lexburg and Denver. The ground was covered with the remains of the splurge battle. Smolsky ordered the six other policemen, who were crammed into the sedan with O'Dreary, to look for clues. They scratched their heads as they scoured the ground around them, occasionally bumping into one another. Suddenly Smolsky let out a triumphant yell.

'Ahaa! Come and take a look at this, O'Dreary.'

O'Dreary ran to the spot where Smolsky was pointing. He crouched down by Smolsky's legs and followed his eyes along the police captain's pointing finger to the 'clue'. O'Dreary looked up at his boss and smiled a smug smile.

'You've cracked it this time, Captain Smolsky.'

Smolsky was a little surprised at this reaction. He'd thought he'd found a clue not a solution. He pushed his hat to the back of his head as movie police captains do.

'I have? What do you see?'

This was a question O'Dreary was not really ready for. He stared at the spot and saw nothing but Smolsky's shoe in the soft mud.

'Tell me, what do you see, O'Dreary?'

'Your foot, Captain.'

Smolsky whipped off his hat in desperation and whacked it across the back of the Irishman's thick head. 'Not my foot, you knucklehead! *Under* my foot. Tyre marks.'

O'Dreary looked again, and, sure enough, under Smolsky's shiny black shoe was the imprint of a tyre from Dandy Dan's bike sedan, pressed out quite clearly in the squelchy mud.

'It's a tyre mark, Captain.'

'Too right it's a tyre mark, you Irish potato head. Get the plaster. We'll take a mould.'

'Sure thing, Captain.'

O'Dreary snapped his fingers at the other policemen to help him. They struggled in the back seat of the sedan for a moment and appeared with a zinc bath filled with plaster. The white liquid slopped around as they staggered with it to the spot where Captain Smolsky was now kneeling. He brushed away the loose pieces of grass from the creases of the tyre imprint. As the tottering policemen backed towards the crouching detective, one of them trod rather awkwardly on a discarded custard pie. It was inevitable. The gooey object threw the unfortunate officer's legs up into the air. The bungling policemen toppled over one another into a pile of arms and legs, and the bath of plaster they were holding tipped upside down, emptying its sloppy white contents over Mrs Smolsky's favourite son.

There should have been all hell let loose, but there wasn't. Instead, there was silence. Even the birds seemed to stop twittering, lest they should be blamed for the mishap. Smolsky gradually stood up. He was covered from head to toe in white plaster that was already beginning to set. He looked like an iced candy figure on top of a birthday cake. The policemen just lay there and stared. No one was brave enough to move, let alone speak. The police captain's face turned scarlet with rage. Not that anyone noticed the colour, as his face was covered in white plaster. Finally a shout—no, not a shout, a strangled scream—came out of Smolsky's mouth.

'Aaah!'

It's difficult to explain this word exactly. It was the kind of word you only see in picture comics—and the kind of sound you might only hear when a rhinoceros accidentally treads on a monkey's foot.

'You idiots!' he yelled. 'Wipe it off before it sets hard.'

The stupefied policemen regained their senses and bumped into one another in their attempts to help their boss.

'Quickly, you jerks! It's beginning to inhibit me,' Smolsky screamed—and the more he screamed, the more the policemen bumbled. And the harder they tried, the harder went Smolsky's plaster overcoat.

Fat Sam had been number one man around the Lower East Side for longer than he could remember. Before him it had been his Uncle Gino—or Stubby Gee as he was affectionately called (or Mad Eyes as he was often, less affectionately, called). Sam would never have admitted it, but Dandy Dan was getting to him, and he could see his precious hoodlum empire crumbling around his ears. Knuckles was all he had left, and when a guy was in a jam like Sam was, he naturally clutched at straws—hence the strange mechanical device that stood on a wooden tripod in the underground garage near Sam's place.

The machine was a hotchpotch of tubes and springs, with a large nickel funnel into which Knuckles was pouring a bucket of splurge. Sam looked at the monstrosity with great optimism, but his sidekick was less certain.

'You sure this is going to work, Boss?' Knuckles queried.

Sam dismissed his henchman's lack of confidence. 'Of course it will! It looks like a splurge gun, doesn't it?'

Knuckles looked at the peculiar contraption in front of him. No one but a sinking man would see any resemblance between this piece of mechanical madness and a snazzy, Dandy Dan Mark One model splurge gun. Sure, it had a barrel that made it look vaguely like a gun. This is probably what prompted Knuckles to reply, 'Well, sort of like a splurge gun, Boss.'

Fat Sam was indignant. 'Anything Dandy Dan can do, Fat Sam can do better. Am I right?'

'Sure thing, Boss.'

Knuckles wasn't about to disagree with him. He was nervous enough as it was—and thoughtlessly cracked his knuckles once more to prove it.

'Don't do that,' Sam snapped.

'Sorry, Boss.'

'Right. Are you ready?'

Knuckles crouched behind the would-be splurge gun and gripped the starter handle that protruded from the side. 'Ready, Boss.'

Sam stood with his feet apart, halfway between the 'gun' and the target—which was a full-size, lifelike cut-out of Dandy Dan.

'O.K. Get set.'

'Set.' Knuckles flexed his fingers around the handle.

Fat Sam narrowed his eyes at the cut-out figure.

'Fire!'

Knuckles cranked the handle for all he was worth and a loud explosion echoed around the garage. Sam ran towards the target to see the damage his new weapon had achieved. There was no sign of a mark—splurge or otherwise—anywhere on it. He smacked Dan's painted face.

'Missed! Oh, well—it's back to the drawing board, Knuckles.'

The fat mobster covered his eyes with his hand as he walked away from the figure. 'What we gonna do, Knuckles?' he muttered.

There was no reply. Sam looked up—and it was then that he saw the results of the explosion. Neither Knuckles nor the machine were in an upright position. The contraption had blown its seams and lay in a smoking, smouldering mess around Knuckles—who was submerged in a gallon or two of white, sticky splurge. Fat Sam's mouth dropped open at the sight. Whatever game it was that everybody was playing, Knuckles had cashed in his chips.

It was at that moment that Fat Sam lost his studied hoodlum cool. He lapsed into the Italian he'd learned on his grandmother's knee and ran to the far end of the garage, half shouting and half weeping. He punched at Dan's painted face, and the wooden cut-out fell backwards with a loud crash that sent clouds of long-settled dust bursting into the atmosphere. Right then, Sam would have been the first to admit he wasn't entirely in control of the situation. But he would also have added that 'us Italians can get a little emotional at times'—and he upended a workbench full of tools on to the floor. The noise of the clattering metal and his desperate shouts could be heard for six blocks. Fat Sam was getting a little emotional.

Meanwhile, back at the intersection of Lexburg and Denver, Smolsky's covering of 'Quick Dri' plaster had lived up to its name and had set to a rigid coat that stiffened Smolsky's body like a dehydrated straightjacket. O'Dreary delicately poked his boss, feet first, into the back of the police car. Smolsky looked less like a precinct detective than like a sort of plaster ornament people stand in their gardens. He yelled at the clumsy police helpers as they tried hard not to bend his stiffened body.

'Careful, you idiots! Go easy, it's cutting into my neck, you clumsy dummy.'

O'Dreary tried to calm his boss down as he got into the driving seat.

'Don't worry, Captain. We'll break you out when we get back to Headquarters.'

The bike sedan pulled off down the track with Smolsky's plaster-splattered head protruding from the back window. But his large, rubber-lipped Polish mouth had been spared the clinging mess and was working overtime to make up for the rest of his imprisoned body.

23. SLUGGERS GYM

The boxer in the ring winced as he took a left hook from his sparring partner, and he clung on illegally in the hope of getting a second breath. It was the first thing Leroy saw as he stepped into Sluggers Gym, and he groaned. He turned on his heels and made straight for the exit, but Bugsy pulled him back inside.

Leroy protested, 'I'm scared, Bugsy. Maybe I'd better stick to digging roads.'

'Nonsense. Your place is here. Wait till you meet Cagey Joe. He'll straighten you out as quick as it takes to count you out in ten.'

Leroy didn't like the comparison. He looked around him at the factory of muscle and sweat. Everywhere he saw fighters—good and bad, promising fighters, has-been fighters, white fighters, black fighters. Everywhere fighters punishing their bodies and punishing the heavy bags like they were their worst enemy. The smell of their sweated labour filled the air and the sound of yelps and grunts made Leroy wince.

Ever since he was little (actually, Leroy had never been little because he weighed fourteen pounds at birth and had put on weight steadily until he'd reached his present bulbous proportions), he'd known he was stronger than the other kids on the block. But with a temperament as cool as Louisiana lemonade and a smile so warm that it made you want to eat him, he'd never really got into fights. That's not to say he hadn't hit people. Occasionally he'd forget his massive weight (and punch). During impromptu football games in the car lot, Leroy would get carried away and half the opposing team would end up picking themselves off the floor, rubbing their sore chins and shaking their dazed heads. Often they wouldn't get up at all until they were brought back to the land of the living with a well-aimed bucket of water.

Leroy had been born in Louisiana, the eighth of eight

strapping children. Even in a family as enormous as Leroy's, a fourteen-pound smiling baby is something of an event. Leroy's father had moved the family north in search of a better job for himself and a better life and future for his eight offspring. They'd moved to Philadelphia first, before making their way to the big apple—New York. Which is where Leroy found himself. A soft, cuddly, teddy bear of a boy in a neighbourhood so tough you could get a Congressional medal for walking the streets after dark. But it hadn't spoiled Leroy. He smiled when he was provoked, and laughed when he was shouted at. There was a kindness from inside him that shone in his eyes and glittered from his pearly white teeth. Also, as they say in Louisiana, he was built like a brick chicken-house, and everyone knew that if you messed around too far with Leroy you were in danger of having the point of your chin punched somewhere back where your ears used to be.

Which is why Bugsy gripped him firmly by the arm and dragged the reluctant lad towards Cagey Joe, who was leaning between the ring ropes, watching the two boxers swapping punches above him. His narrow, evil eyes were trained on his fighters, and he blinked, and twisted his face, as punches flew, missed and connected. As he dropped his concentration for a minute, he noticed Bugsy and Leroy, and threw open his arms to greet his old friend.

'Bugsy! How you been, man?'

'Swell, Cagey Joe. Swell. And you?'

'For me, good—but for this bunch of punch bags . . .'

He twisted his nose again as he threw a disapproving look at the two fighters who seemed to be belting the life out of one another. Bugsy pulled Leroy forward.

'Cagey Joe, I want you to meet the next heavyweight champion. Leroy, meet Cagey Joe. Cagey Joe, meet Leroy Smith.'

Cagey Joe turned his piercing slit eyes in Leroy's direction. The stare was evil enough to frighten the boy into politely taking off his hat. Cagey Joe circled slowly.

'Ever been in the ring before, boy?'

'Nope.'

'So you wanna be a fighter, huh?'

'Nope.'

Leroy was falling back on his usual witty dialogue. Cagey Joe looked at Bugsy, somewhat puzzled.

95

'Sure he does,' said Bugsy quickly. 'Look at those fists. Did you ever see such fists? Hit it, Leroy.'

Bugsy held up his palmed hand. Leroy made a fist that looked more like a bag of walnuts than a handful of knuckles. He threw it in the direction of Bugsy's open hand, and it connected with an almighty slap that made Bugsy wonder if he'd ever hold a pool cue again.

'See what I mean?' said Bugsy, through gritted teeth. 'A champion. A born champion.'

Cagey Joe's eyes narrowed even more and beamed their way into Leroy's face like powerful searchlights. Cagey Joe had coached more champions than anyone in New York and he knew boxing talent when he saw it. The timing of Leroy's punch, the casual way it was thrown, and the strength with which it hit the target were all taken in by those reptilian eyes. He blinked, and the information was recorded and stored away in the boxing computer which was the back of his head. He walked round Leroy once more. This time, he squeezed the boy's muscular arms, and noticed the way his strong neck muscles grew out of his hefty shoulders. There was no doubt about it. Cagey Joe was impressed.

'What's your name again, kid?'

'Leroy Smith.'

Bugsy, nursing his sore fingers, which felt like a hand of last week's bananas, sensed that Cagey Joe had bitten the bait.

'With you showing him the ropes, Cagey Joe, he could be a champion in no time.'

Cagey Joe shrugged his shoulders and said, 'O.K. I'll give him a try. But I tell you now, he'll be no good unless he's got "it".'

'It?' puzzled Leroy.

Bugsy explained. ' "It" is what makes you special in the ring, Leroy. It's the difference between being a slugger and a champion. "It" is the difference between being a champ and being a bottom-of-the-bill filler at a local charity show.'

'It's what makes a fighter special,' chipped in Joe. 'If you haven't got "it", then you haven't got it.'

Leroy was a little confused, but before he could understand what they were talking about, he had been pushed towards the swing doors that led to the changing rooms.

An enormous fighter, at least a foot taller than Leroy, leaned over the ropes and yelled, 'Let me have him, Joe. I'll make mincemeat out of him.'

Leroy had never really imagined himself chopped up on a butcher's slab for twenty cents a pound, and the thought set his adam's apple nervously bobbing around inside his throat. But Cagey Joe thrust some boots and a pair of red silk boxing shorts into his hands and pushed him the last yard into the changing room.

The room was damp and dark, and Leroy tripped a few times climbing into the baggy shorts. Finally, he made his entrance. As he pushed the swing doors open into the brightly lit gym, he felt like an ancient Roman gladiator hitting daylight as he stepped from the tunnel into the Coliseum. There was silence as he climbed into the ring. Bugsy tied his gloves tightly around his wrists for him and slapped him on the back for encouragement. Then Cagey Joe yanked at the bell rope and the metal ball inside crashed against the brass to start the first round.

The tall fighter came out of his corner and met Leroy centre ring. He was even meaner-looking up here, thought Leroy, who was manoeuvring his large lips to try and cope with the awkward gumshield that protected his teeth. The tall fighter flicked out three punches in a row that picked off Leroy's head like it was a melon on a stick. Leroy blinked, and the two fighters circled one another. The tall boy let go a series of one-two combination punches that mainly hit Leroy on the side of his ample arms, which were dug into his sides to protect his porky frame. Bugsy watched through the ropes with the rest of the fighters, who had stopped to watch the contest—or the no-contest, as they all presumed.

Bugsy was getting a little anxious, because so far Leroy hadn't even thrown a punch. The other fighters smiled, waiting for the knockout blow. It came the very next punch—except that it was Leroy who threw it. He ducked a wild swing from the tall boy and let go a left hook that caught his opponent under the chin and lifted him a clear two feet in the air before he collapsed in a heap on the canvas—out cold.

The spectators were dumbfounded. Bugsy clapped his hands with joy, and Leroy looked at the left glove that had K.O.'d his opponent with as much surprise as every-

97

D

B.M.

body else. Cagey Joe shrugged his shoulders and had to admit. 'He's got it.'

Leroy smiled his blazing white, toothy smile. He'd known it all along.

24. POYSANALLY

In the disused garage, the illicit still bubbled and steamed away through a maze of pipes and containers, until the dark, treacle-like liquid finally poured out into a wooden barrel. A boy in brown overalls and a dirty, wrap-around apron operated the tap that trickled the sarsaparilla, by way of a funnel, into bottles. They were neatly stacked in rows, and full crates were piled, six high, ready for collection. This was where Fat Sam made all his illegal drinks for his speakeasy, and it was a surprise to no one—except to the man who operated the still—that this would be the place Dandy Dan's gang would strike next.

The garage door was smashed practically off its hinges and crashed down on to the floor. The still operator jumped up in fright. He wasn't the bravest person at the best of times, and the sight of Chinese Benny Lee rushing at him, screaming a war cry from his distant oriental past, was more than he could take. His teeth chattered and his knees knocked like Spanish castanets. Benny Lee was followed by Yonkers and Shoulders, and then by Bronx Charlie, who pinned the unfortunate operator against the wall with his splurge gun. The rest of the gang caused havoc with the still. Yonkers and Chinese Benny chopped at the barrel lids and upended them until the contents gushed all over the garage floor. They threw the full bottles at the wall—and the glass smashed into a million pieces, spreading the thick sarsaparilla liquid across the dry bricks. Shoulders wielded a large axe at an enormous wooden storage vat, and the hole he split open sent a river of sarsaparilla flowing through the garage.

In seconds, they had finished. Bronx Charlie wound a rope around the boggle-eyed operator and tied his hands behind him with tight knots. The rest of the gang stopped briefly to eye their destructive handiwork, allowed themselves a chuckle, and then splashed out over the door which they had stampeded only minutes before.

The petrified still operator edged himself slowly towards his desk. He banged the side of it with his head and the stick phone toppled on to the floor. He crawled over to it, as well as the tight ropes would allow, and managed to dial a number.

In Fat Sam's office, the secret phone rang in the desk drawer. Sam yanked it open with his podgy hand and snatched the receiver from the cradle.

'Hello?'

'They got to the still, Boss. The whole lot's gone.'

Fat Sam took the news badly. He'd known something like this could happen, but he had always put it into the corner of his mind where people forget things they don't want to think about. His red face drained to a milky white.

'No. Not the sarsaparilla racket, too? You'd better get round here right away.'

'I can't, Boss.'

'Why not?'

'I'm all tied up, Boss.'

'I don't care how busy you are. Get round here right away.'

Fat Sam crashed down the phone. He put his head in his hands and muttered low Italian moans. But there was no one to hear them. He was on his own. He would have moaned even more if he'd known what was happening on the other side of town.

Shoulders' huge, powerful legs pounded the pedals up and down and the hoods' bike sedan reached an alarming speed before it crashed into the wooden gates of the Stacetto Brothers' grocery yard.

Under the impact, the gates splintered and cracked, and pieces of wood flew in all directions. The two grocery men, who were loading their truck in the yard, were taken completely by surprise. Dandy Dan's hoods threw them into a corner. Piles of crates were toppled over and the hoods began trampling on the green vegetables that spilled out

99

across the floor. The grocery men were powerless to do anything.

It didn't take long for Dan's men to do their work. In two minutes flat the grocery yard looked like an elephant had run amok through it. The hoods jumped into their car and reversed out into the street. They wore big, satisfied, Cheshire cat smiles on their faces—which is more than could be said for Fat Sam when he heard the news.

He listened with utter disbelief as the squeaky voice on the phone gave him the sad tidings. Tallulah had joined him, and sat on the corner of his desk, painting her nails with a red varnish that perfectly matched the colour of her glossy lips. Sam gulped, and reached for his orange juice cocktail.

'Not the grocery racket too? Oh, no. That's terrible. Terrible. All right. O.K., sure. No, I'm sure you did your best. Go home and get washed up, O.K. 'Bye.' Sam gently put down the receiver. He stroked the rim of his cocktail glass and stared sadly into open air. He croaked as he spoke. 'That's the whole empire gone, Tallulah. You hear me? Everything. And they'll be coming here next.'

Tallulah breathed on her nails to dry them. She really couldn't have cared less. Sam continued to stroke his glass nervously.

'There's only one thing for it. You'll have to get him to help me.'

'Who? The Lone Ranger?'

'No, you dumb dora. Bugsy Malone. Call him.'

Tallulah picked up the stick phone carefully so as not to spoil her nail varnish. She dialled with the end of Fat Sam's desk pen. He muttered to himself as she did so.

'I'm in trouble. Real trouble. And all I've got for company is a female comedian.'

Tallulah tucked the phone ear piece neatly under her blonde hair, taking extra care not to disturb her curls. Not that there was much hope of that. At Madame Monzani's Hair Parlour on 2nd Avenue, they pasted curls down for good, and boasted that even a hurricane wouldn't put a hair out of place.

The phone rang at Bugsy's end for some minutes.

'There's no answer.'

'Then you'll have to get him *personally*,' Fat Sam snapped. His girlfriend never ever reacted to his rudeness.

Well, not so as you'd notice. Her eyebrows would make the teeniest of movements, which said all, should you be close enough to catch it.

Sam repeated his command. 'You deaf or somethin'? I said you'll have to get him to help me *personally*.' He pronounced it '*poysanally*'.

Tallulah looked down at him through her eyelashes. 'Personally?'

'Poysanally!'

'Poysanally.'

Tallulah picked up her fox shoulder fur and walked to the door. 'So long, lover boy. Take it easy.'

She blew him a kiss and pulled the door closed behind her. She was on her way to Bugsy Malone's apartment where she would get his undivided attention. Poysanally.

25. MR. BIG

Bugsy whistled to himself as he ran up the stairs to his apartment. Correction—for apartment, read room with an alcove to wash in. It wasn't a fancy place, or a snazzy neighbourhood, but it suited him—and at one dollar ninety it suited his pocket. As he turned the corner on the stairs, he passed his upstairs neighbour with her child. He raised his hat to the lady and smiled at the little girl. The courtesy to the mother was genuine enough but the smile was false. The little horror whose hand she held had kept Bugsy awake too many nights with her screaming for him to like her.

He moved toward his own door—and suddenly pulled himself up dead in his tracks. The door was ajar. He could see a crack of light spreading across the carpet outside. He stepped softly backwards towards a small cupboard at the end of the hall. In it he found a small, sawn-off broom which he grasped tightly in his hands. He eased back towards the door. Taking a deep breath, he burst through it —and tripped over a well-placed suitcase which launched him headlong into the room. He landed by a pair of shoes.

A pair of ladies' shoes. The roller-blind snapped up and light flooded in, filling the room with sunshine. Bugsy looked up from the shoes and saw that they belonged to Tallulah.

'I like my men at my feet,' she said.

Bugsy smiled with relief, helped himself up and sat down in the wickerwork chair at the side of his bed.

'What are you doing here, Tallulah?'

'I've got a message for you.'

'What's wrong with Western Union?'

'I thought you'd . . . er . . . like the company.'

Bugsy gulped with embarrassment. Tallulah was always too quick for him. 'When I get lonely, I walk around Central Park,' he joked.

Tallulah rather enjoyed seeing him sweat.

'You gonna fix me a drink?'

'I'm right out.'

She gave up. 'Come on. I'll buy you a drink.'

'Where?'

'Fat Sam's place.'

Bugsy suddenly had visions of being caught talking to Sam's girl in Sam's place. That was madness . . . That meant a knuckle sandwich at least from Fat Sam, not to mention a broken nose. And Bugsy told himself he was too pretty to have his face messed up. It wouldn't be fair to the world.

'Won't Fat Sam be there?'

'He sure will.'

Bugsy couldn't believe his ears. He wasn't going to risk having his neck broken.

'Maybe I'll stay home.'

Tallulah sighed heavily and picked up her fur. 'Don't flatter yourself, Tiger. He's the one who wants to see you, not me.' She straightened his tie and brushed a mock fist across his nose. 'Come on. Let's go, before your suspenders strangle you.'

Bugsy blew out a deep sigh of relief as Tallulah moved towards the door. He picked up his hat and used it as a fan. In the last few minutes he'd got a little hot under the collar.

In the speakeasy, Fizzy slopped water over the floor and whistled as he slid his mop to and fro. Behind the bar, the barman was polishing glasses. Fat Sam walked slowly up to the counter. He shouted at Fizzy without even looking at him. 'Quit whistling, Fizzy. It makes me edgy.'

'Sure thing, Boss.'

Sam leaned heavily on the bar, took a toothpick from a glass and snapped it viciously between his fingers. He beckoned the barman with a click of his fingers. The barman stopped his glass-polishing immediately.

'Yes, Boss?'

'Get me a double on the rocks.'

'Sure thing, Boss.'

The barman scooped crushed ice into a glass and pulled the cork out of the 'green special' bottle. Then he made a big mistake.

The flower in Sam's lapel was a bedraggled, pathetic specimen of horticulture, two days overdue for being thrown away. The barman sniggered. Fat Sam fixed him with a dangerous glare.

'So what's funny, buster? You find me amusing?'

'No, Boss . . . I wasn't smiling at you. Honest I wasn't.'

'You find my suit amusing or something?'

'No, Boss. It was . . . it was . . . your flower.' The barman pointed nervously to the drooping snowdrop.

Fat Sam looked down at it and smiled. At least, he seemed to smile. 'Oh, yeah. It's kinda droopy, ain't it?' He beamed as he said it and the barman also started to smile.

'Yeah, a little, Boss,' he giggled nervously. He thought it was strange to find Sam in such a good mood. Sam laughed even louder.

'In fact, it's very droopy!' Sam bellowed with laughter and so did the barman. He couldn't believe his luck. No one had ever got on this well with the boss before. Maybe he was in for promotion.

'Yeah, Boss. Very droopy,' he giggled.

Sam took the floppy flower from his lapel and handed it to the barman.

'Here, hold it a minute, will you? It needs a little water.'

Still smiling, the unsuspecting barman took the flower in his hand. Sam picked up the jug of water that stood on the counter and threw the entire contents at the flower—with the result that it, and the barman, were completely drenched. Sam grabbed the boy by the scruff of the neck and yanked him across the counter, scattering empty bottles and glasses. Suspended inches from Sam's nose, he caught, head on, the verbal broadside that spouted from Sam's mouth.

'Now don't let me see you laughing at me again, you hear? I'll ram that smile right down your throat. I'm Fat Sam. Don't ever forget that. Number one man. Top dog. Mr Big. Always have been. Always will be. Now get out of here.'

The barman bounced from side to side as he was propelled by Fat Sam in the direction of the exit.

The fat hoodlum brushed his hands down his suit and poured himself another drink. He was still the number one man—the Mr Big around this joint who always managed to keep his head up. But not for long—because he walked into Fizzy's shiny wet floor, broke the world record for the heavy fall, and landed on his backside with a thundering crunch that would have bruised him more had he not been blessed with a back-end that nature had thoughtfully built to take such shocks. Fizzy was terrified. He blurted out a warning that was as pointless as it was late.

'Be careful, Boss. The floor is wet.'

Quite simply, Sam went mad. He grabbed a table and pulled himself up. Fizzy didn't waste a second. He scuttled around the table in the opposite direction. Sam cleared the upturned chairs with one sweep of his hand. They clattered around Fizzy's ears, but he still kept running. Sam ran after him and up the stairs to the stage. If he'd caught the little janitor there's no telling what he would have done with him, but, luckily for Fizzy, at that moment the door opened, and in came Tallulah and Bugsy.

'Here he is, honey. As promised.'

Fat Sam stopped, and his face turned from rage to pleasure. 'Bugsy, how are you? How you been?'

'Fine. And you?'

'Oh, a little difficulty at the moment, Bugsy. Why don't you pull up a chair and sit down? Tallulah, honey, fix him a drink, will you?'

'What's your pleasure, Bugsy?' said Tallulah with a smile.

'Special-on-the-rocks, Tallulah, please.'

Bugsy and Sam pulled up chairs. Sam pushed his closer to Bugsy and dropped his voice to an intimate whisper.

'Bugsy, I need your help. I'm in a jam. Dandy Dan's breathing down my neck and any minute now he'll be taking over my entire organisation.'

Bugsy found it hard to believe. After all, there was still the speakeasy. Bugsy could see it with his own eyes and in the evenings he could see how much money it made, too. He said, 'You've still got all this.'

Sam replied with a gesture that could only have been learned in Naples.

'Not if Dandy Dan gets his way. I won't have a dime for a shoe-shine.'

'Nothing?'

'Not a red cent.'

Tallulah returned with the drinks. She put Bugsy's down in front of him and then pulled herself up a chair.

'Tallulah,' Sam said sharply, 'Can you leave us for a minute? This is men's talk.'

Tallulah stroked Bugsy's hair. 'It's all right. I'm un-shockable.'

But Sam was insistent. 'Tallulah, go fix your make-up.'

'I've already fixed it.'

'Then go and make yourself even more beautiful than you already are.'

'But you know that's impossible.'

'Tallulah.' Sam was getting angry. He glared at her with a look that could have cut a man in half. It bounced off Tallulah. She stood up.

'All right. All right. I'll go manicure my gloves.'

She stormed across the speakeasy floor and up the stairs to the girls' dressing room.

Fat Sam turned to Bugsy. 'Bugsy, I need help. My gang's all gone. My friends don't want to know me. My business is in ruins. I'm a wreck. In short, Bugsy, I need you.'

Bugsy was more than a little taken aback.

'Me? Why me?'

' 'Cause you're no mug. You've got brains up there, not pretzels.' He tapped his head to make it quite clear where he admired brains.

Bugsy was not impressed. He'd spent his whole life keeping out of trouble and he saw no reason to get in-volved now.

'No, it's not my line.'

Fat Sam leaned even closer and held him firmly, if not

affectionately, by the arm. 'Help me, and I'll give you two hundred bucks to go with the two hundred I already gave you.'

But Bugsy shrugged once more. 'Impossible.'

This surprised Sam, who said, 'I thought you were smart?'

'Impossible, because I've already lost the first two hundred.'

Sam was amazed. 'Have I misjudged this Bugsy Malone?' he thought.

'You lost two hundred bucks? Gambling?'

'No, I was mugged.'

Fat Sam shrugged with his face, as only Italians can. He was as sympathetic as a hood could be who regarded mugging in the same way as a world series baseball player regards a pitch and catch match in the local park. Sam said nothing more and got out his wallet. He peeled off dollar after dollar, counting them on to the table. 'Two hundred green ones, plus the two hundred you lost.'

Bugsy couldn't believe his eyes. 'Four hundred bucks!'

Sam was impatient. 'Do we have a deal?'

Bugsy felt the crisp, new, green and black notes crackle between his fingers. He whistled quietly to himself as he weighed up the price of keeping his independence against the possibility of those precious dollars vanishing into Fat Sam's pocket, lost to him forever.

'Well?' Sam pushed him.

Bugsy couldn't resist. 'You have a deal.'

They shook hands and smiled at one another. It was then that the telephone rang. Tallulah answered it upstairs.

'Bugsy, it's for you. It's Blousey.'

'Excuse me a minute, Sam.'

'Sure thing, Bugsy. Take your time. Use the phone all you want. Be my guest. Phone home. Phone Europe. Phone wherever you please. If Dandy Dan takes over this place he'll have to pay the phone bill. Ha ha ha.' Sam's laugh fooled no one.

Bugsy counted the money as he walked up the stairs. Tallulah blew him a kiss as she handed him the phone. Bugsy smiled coyly. He stroked his eyebrow with his finger as a token gesture of embarrassment. But he also was fooling no one. Certainly not Tallulah.

'Hello, Blousey?'

Blousey had waited patiently. She had sat on a stool by the phone in her apartment house hallway for a good twenty minutes before she'd plucked up courage to phone the speakeasy. The wind zipped down the New York streets and rattled the ill-fitting window panes, sending a draught whistling past Blousey's door. She had wrapped herself in the pink and blue dressing gown her Auntie Mary from Wisconsin had made for her. It kept her warm and made her look even sadder, flopping as it did in neat folds around her thin legs and slippered feet. She'd flicked through the Manhattan and Bronx phone book in search of Bugsy's favourite pool hall. She'd even left a message with the janitor's wife in his building. In desperation, she'd rung the speakeasy. Tallulah's voice on the other end of the phone was not a welcome sound. 'Sure he's here. I'll get him for you, honey.'

Blousey couldn't pretend it didn't hurt. She had set her heart on getting out of New York and away to the coast and fame. She'd always been a dreamer. And while her fantasies seemed so much nicer than her real life, she saw no reason to make excuses for it. Maybe Bugsy being nice to her was a fantasy too. A daydream that would disappear when the rumble of a heavy truck or the elevated railway snapped her out of it. She didn't have to wait more than a minute for Bugsy to answer, but it seemed like a week and it made her realise how much she wanted him to be genuine.

'Hello, Blousey?'

'Bugsy? Is that you? What are you doing there?'

'Just business.'

'With Tallulah?'

'With Fat Sam.'

'Did you get the tickets?'

'No, not yet. Something's come up.'

He saw no point in lying to her, though he didn't want to hurt her. But to someone with hopes as big as Blousey's, one small step backwards to a normal person is a whole flight of stairs. She took it on the chin.

'But you promised me. You promised me.'

'I know, but Hollywood can wait a couple of days, can't it?'

This also seemed reasonable to Bugsy. Ever since Jesse Lasky had put up that shed to make De Mille's '*Squaw Man*' twenty years ago, Hollywood had grown and sprawled too far for anyone to believe such a tinselled monster could disappear overnight.

Blousey took this second blow on the chin, too.

'You had no intention of taking me to Hollywood.'

'I do. Look, there's just something I've got to do first.'

At this moment, Tallulah came on the scene with Bugsy's drink. It was impeccable timing by the smart blonde lady—but for Bugsy it was as well-timed as an iceberg floating into an ocean liner. Tallulah leaned on his shoulder and whispered in his ear, soft enough to make the hairs on the back of Bugsy's neck stand on end, and loud enough for Blousey to catch.

'You rat! You promised me!'

Bugsy pulled the phone away from his head as the shriek of Blousey's voice vibrated his inner eardrum like rain on a tin roof.

'Look, trust me, will you? I'll call you.' He replaced the earpiece in its holder. Pushing his hat to the back of his head, he took a consolation sip of his drink.

Blousey put down the phone and leaned sadly against the wall. Maybe it was just a dream after all.

26. TRAPPED

Stones would do it. Leroy's window was on the first storey at the front of the house. Bugsy had leaned on his bell for five minutes but still couldn't wake him up. He scooped up a handful of loose gravel from the gutter and tossed it for all he was worth at Leroy's window. It worked. As soon as the stones made noisy contact with the glass, a light went on. Leroy pulled up the window and poked his sleepy head out.

'Who's there?' he said, as his stubby fingers rubbed the sleep out of his eyes.

'It's me. Bugsy. Get dressed and come down. We've got a job!' Bugsy tried not to laugh at Leroy's rather peculiar, baggy, striped pyjamas.

'You've got me a crack at the title already?'

'No, this is a different type of job.'

Leroy wasn't interested in work at the best of times, let alone at this hour.

'I'm tired. Come back in the morning.'

'There's two hundred dollars in it for you.'

The change in Leroy was miraculous. His sticky, sleepy eyes clanked open like the tumblers in a fruit machine. Leroy's pappy always used to say, 'When you're down on your luck and there's nothing but clouds on the horizon, then a prayer, a song, and a few bucks is like a ray of sunshine.' To Leroy, the possibility of earning two hundred dollars was like an entire heat-wave summer. He retreated inside so fast that he misjudged the height of the window and knocked his head heavily on the wooden frame. He rubbed his granite skull and the pain went. The window frame had no such luck.

Leroy and Bugsy crawled through the overgrown bushes at the edge of the lawn outside Dandy Dan's mansion and stared at the truck parked in the drive. They had managed to avoid the guards on the front gate by crawling through a hole in the wire fence. Leroy had torn the hole himself—pulling the wire apart as easily as someone ripping out a detachable lining from a raincoat.

Bugsy held Leroy back with his arm and ducked down. Leroy copied him, although he didn't know why.

'We've got to get closer.'

The two crawled along on their tummies until they were scarcely twenty feet from the truck. Bugsy suddenly saw what Dan's men were guarding so closely.

'Splurge guns!'

His whispered explanation took Leroy by surprise. He quickly looked about him, expecting to be held up.

'Where?'

'In the crates, stupid. Look what it says on the side of the truck.'

'I can't.'

'Can't you read?'

'Sure. It's just that I'm a little short-sighted. Who does it say?'

Bugsy read out the words painted on the side of the truck, which were also stencilled on the wooden boxes loaded into it.

'The Splurge Imports Company Inc. Dock 17, East River.'

'That must be where they keep the guns.'

Leroy was no Sherlock Holmes—or Doctor Watson, come to that—but he wasn't stupid. Well, not very stupid.

Suddenly Bugsy saw something else. Two burly guards, dressed in evil-looking baseball catchers' masks and wielding baseball clubs, had just turned the corner towards them.

'Look out, Leroy.'

The two boys crawled back into the bushes as fast as they could. As they emerged on the other side, they saw that their path was blocked by another pair of baseball guards. Leroy turned to Bugsy, who was thinking fast. Leroy was grateful for that.

'What are we gonna do, Bugsy?'

'We're going to have to make a run for it—there's too many of them. Ready?'

'Ready?'

They pounded down the narrow, high-hedged path that led them back to the hole in the fence. But in their hurry they missed a thin trip wire that stretched across the lane. Leroy's boot caught it first. His feet were thrown in the air and he did a belly flop dive on to the gravel. The trip wire yanked another wire that pulled a handle that set the alarms going. In seconds, there was pandemonium. The air was filled with the jarring, ear-splitting sounds of bells, klaxon hooters and barking dogs. From every direction, guards descended on the two boys. Bugsy was knocked out by the first swing of a baseball bat, but Leroy managed to floor a good half-dozen of them before he, too, had butterflies fluttering in his head from a K.O. slug.

The hoods went through Bugsy's pockets and took out two Greyhound tickets. One of them read them out aloud.

'You've gotta believe it, fellahs. Listen to this. Two tickets to guess where? Hollywood.'

The rest of the guards laughed—and the tickets landed in a screwed-up ball next to Bugsy's head.

'The only stars he'll be seeing are between the eyes.'

It was a fair description, because, apart from the butterflies and the odd goldfish floating above him, stars were all Bugsy was seeing. He hadn't even told Blousey he'd bought the tickets. Now she'd never know.

Blousey sat on the end of her bed and clicked open the brass fasteners on the battered leather bag her Uncle Digby had loaned her when she first left for New York. She'd got a little ahead of herself and started to pack for Hollywood, which was a mistake, because it made the situation all the more painful when she unpacked. As she reached into the bag, she saw the nickelodeon viewer that Bugsy had given her. She rubbed the tortoiseshell with her sleeve until it shone like new. The Hollywood stars were still there when she held it up to the light, but somehow they didn't shine so brightly now. They seemed so far away.

She should never have thrown in her job at the speakeasy. It had taken her nearly six months to get a job and only two weeks to give it back.

She dropped her head in embarrassment as she walked along the corridor to Fat Sam's office. The other girls smiled to themselves as she passed them. Loretta, Dotty and Tillie almost bumped into her as she turned the corner.

'Hi, Blousey. Miss your train?'

'Hi, Blousey. What happened?'

'Your guy let you down?'

Their questions had no hope of getting answers. Blousey's attention was clearly somewhere else. She rapped hard on the door marked 'S. Stacetto. Private'. Fat Sam opened the door gingerly. With no hoods around him, he was a little careful whom he opened the door to. He was relieved to find it was Blousey.

'Yes, honey. What can I do for you?'

Blousey forced herself to ask. 'I was wondering if I could have my job back?'

Fat Sam was in a good mood. He felt strength in numbers and was very pleased to have her around.

'Sure, honey. Go right in. Everyone's welcome. The more the merrier.'

He blew her a kiss with his frankfurter sausage fingers.

111

But she missed it, because her head had dropped down again. As she went into the girls' room, she passed Tallulah and Velma who were buffing up their nails.

'Hi, Blousey. How you been?' they asked in unison. But even the two of them together couldn't get through to Blousey. She ignored them both. Velma let out a sympathetic sigh.

'Did you ever see a broad carry a torch so high?'

'Yeah, the Statue of Liberty.'

The words were scarcely out of Tallulah's mouth before the girls' room door slammed in her face. Tallulah shrugged her slinky shoulders and walked away. If anyone had looked close enough they would have seen that she was smiling.

27. ESCAPE

The white blur waved back and forth in the attic at the top of Dandy Dan's mansion. Bugsy blinked to focus his eyes, and the white blur turned into an electric light bulb that swung freely on its flex. He looked around him. Although his head was pounding like a ceremonial kettledrum, he quickly took in the situation.

He was tied to a chair which was also tied to Leroy, who was in a similar position. And they were sitting in their underclothes. Evidently Dandy Dan had taken the precaution of removing their suits to discourage any escape.

Leroy also blinked his way back to reality. He had been going through nightmares where goldfish swallowed goldfish and doors opened to other doors and then to sky, which left him floating in mid-air, where he was finally gobbled up by another goldfish. Leroy was glad he had come to. He preferred a bruised head to being swallowed by a goldfish any day of the week.

Leroy twisted and heaved, and managed to ease the ropes that tied him. Bugsy felt something gnawing into his wrists.

'What are you doing, Leroy?'

'Untying the knots with my teeth. I saw it in a movie once.'

'You did?'

'Sure.'

'Mind you don't go hurting my wrists now.'

'What about my *teeth?*'

They both laughed, but, sure enough, Leroy was having some success. His teeth were big enough, after all. He could bite a cap off a Coke bottle as easily as anyone else bit off a piece of Hershey bar.

In Dandy Dan's drawing room, the string quartet continued their disregard for Mozart by murdering yet another piece of his music. Dan himself was being fitted for a new suit. The arms were tacked on with loose stitches, and the be-spectacled tailor drew meaningful lines on the grey pin-striped material with waxed chalk. Dan stood motionless, staring at his favourite person in the mirror.

There was a knock on the door, and in came Bronx Charlie, his hat held respectfully in his hands. Dan spoke without moving. He was so pinned up by his tailor that he probably couldn't move anyway.

'What is it, Bronx Charlie?'

'Er . . . I was wondering what you wanted us to do with these two guys we caught, Boss.'

'I haven't decided yet, Bronx Charlie.'

'Shall I come back, Boss?'

Dan would have stroked his moustache with his fore-finger—as he always did when he felt superior—if he'd been able to bend his arm. But he merely said, 'Give me an hour to think up something. Something particularly nasty.' And he tugged at the pinned-up grey sleeve, which ripped away from its stitching as Bronx Charlie backed out of the room.

The string quartet were oblivious to the conversation and carried on struggling through their musical piece. Up in heaven, Mozart was probably sitting with his fingers in his ears.

Leroy had made a very good job of undoing Bugsy's ropes, and Bugsy returned the favour by undoing his. Once free, Bugsy ran to the room's single exit, the door. He pushed on

113

it and twisted the handle, but was not surprised to find that he could not open it.

'Locked.'

Leroy stood in the middle of the room, thoughtful, but not exactly alight with brilliant suggestions. Bugsy looked around the empty attic. An old chest, a packing case, the two chairs they had been tied to, and a few old discarded picture frames were all that was in it. He looked up to where the light was coming from and saw a narrow window in the ceiling.

'The skylight, Leroy. Try the skylight.'

Leroy didn't need any more encouragement. He turned over the packing case and placed a bentwood chair on top of it. With great courage, but not a great deal of agility, he hauled his tubby frame on to the wobbly chair. Bugsy watched as his fat friend reached for the iron bars that stretched across the skylight, and began to pull with all his considerable strength. But the bars had little respect for Leroy's muscles and refused to budge.

'It's no good, Bugsy. It won't move.'

As Leroy gave one last tug, the chair on which he was dangerously balanced tottered off the edge of the box—and he was left hanging in mid-air. Bugsy saw the chair topple, and yelled, 'Look out, Leroy! Hang on, hang on.'

Leroy obeyed—but the bars didn't and his ridiculous weight succeeded where his amazing strength had failed. In seconds, not only had the bars been pulled wholly out of the ceiling, but the entire skylight, frame and all, collapsed around Leroy's ears.

Bugsy helped Leroy out of the mangled mess. The falling dust filled the room and was so thick Bugsy could hardly see his pal. When he did, he nearly split his long johns laughing.

'Leroy, look at your face!'

Leroy's face was completely covered in white dust. He put his fingers to his chin to see what Bugsy was laughing at. The white smear on his hand prompted a rare Leroy joke.

'Maybe I'll be able to get a job now.'

Bugsy laughed even more while he helped Leroy to his feet and stood the chair upright. Above them, an enormous hole gaped where the window had been.

'Come on, Leroy. Let's get out of here.'

The skylight led on to a flat roof that had the fortunate advantage of being served by a fire escape. The metal staircase led the two boys conveniently down on to the back lawns of Dandy Dan's mansion. Once on the ground, they ran for all they were worth into the trees.

At a stream that led away from the house they stopped. Two hoods were patrolling a small bridge which Bugsy knew led to the main road out. He grabbed hold of Leroy's arm and pulled his friend into the water. Leroy was dumb-founded—and giggled as the water came up to his waist. Under cover of the bridge, the two escapers silently edged away into the darkness of the woods and safety. Silent, that is, apart from the occasional squeal from Leroy as the cold water seeped into his long johns.

28. SPLURGE INC.

At Dock 17, the sign painted on the bricks in six foot high letters read '*SPLURGE INC.*' and told Bugsy and Leroy that this must be Splurge Imports, the house of the guns. Outside was further evidence, for baseball guards patrolled everywhere, scouring the dock for likely intruders. Bugsy and Leroy tucked themselves down behind a row of olive oil barrels and viewed the proceedings with dismay.

Bugsy counted in a whisper. 'Two guards on the door, two on the roof, two at the rear, two on the pier. What we gonna do, Leroy?'

'Go home?'

'There *must* be a way in.'

Leroy was a little more realistic than Bugsy. He still had a bump on his head as big as a gull's egg from the swipe of one of the guards' baseball bat, and wasn't about to slug it out with them again in a hurry.

'Don't be stupid, Bugsy. We'll never get through that lot.'

'I guess you're right.'

The two crawled along behind the barrels until they were safely out of sight of the guards on Dock 17. Both of them looked a little dejected as they walked along the dockside, dwarfed by the huge cargo ships which seemed to make their problem all the bigger. They turned at the end of the wharf and took a short cut down a narrow, cobbled alleyway. Bugsy was the first to speak.

'What we gonna do, Leroy?'

'We need a few more men.'

Bugsy nodded in agreement. The more he thought of the possibility of taking on the tough baseball guards, the more he thought they needed more than the few men that Leroy had suggested.

'We need an army.'

'There ain't no armies around here, Bugsy.'

As Leroy made this remark, almost as if on cue, they heard a low rumbling sound from the dark, narrow entrance they were at that moment passing. Bugsy looked at Leroy. Inside the entrance was a narrow flight of stairs. The two boys began to climb them. The monotonous rumble became louder as they neared the door at the top. It was a constant, almost desperate sound. Unworldly. Leroy's eyes flashed white on the dark staircase. At the top, Bugsy pushed open the door and the noise rose to its full pitch.

On the other side was a mission hall soup kitchen, with long rows of wooden tables. Dozens of desolate, ragged, down-and-outs queued for free bowls of soup and a portion of bread at a counter where three plump ladies were ladling out bowl after bowl of a steaming brown liquid. It looked horried, but tasted like roast turkey to the wretched down-and-outs. Above them, painted across a large wooden beam, was a banner that read, *'The Lord will provide'*. And Father O'Grady, the priest who ran the mission, made sure the Lord provided the earthly soup the down-and-outs' empty bellies appreciated so much.

As they filed past the giant saucepan, each hobo let out a low miserable moan that multiplied into a chant. 'Down, down, down and out. Down, down, down and out,' it seemed to say. The dissolute, shabby bunch dragged their feet and shuffled through the dust that lay thickly on the floorboards.

Bugsy and Leroy looked at one another. Neither said anything but they both knew what the other was thinking. Here was the ready-made army they needed. But these

116

were all boys down on their luck, with broken lives and broken spirits. Without a dime in their pockets or a dream or a hope amongst the lot of them.

Bugsy and Leroy walked up and down the lines, shaking life back into the wretched, luckless bodies. One by one, the down-and-outs listened to their arguments. And one by one they were won round, until Bugsy's army was forty strong and Father O'Grady and his three plump helpers had lost all their regular customers.

The down-and-out's feet made a loud scuffing sound as they edged along the narrow alleyway towards the Splurge Inc. wharf on Dock 17. Bugsy hissed at them to be quiet and urged them to cling to the wall in case the baseball guards caught sight of them. The forty boys ducked down behind the olive oil barrels where Bugsy and Leroy had first found refuge. Bugsy shielded his eyes from the sun and reviewed the situation.

'Right. There they are. All ready for the taking. Get Babyface.'

Leroy, at Bugsy's side, turned to the down-and-out next to him and repeated Bugsy's command. 'Get Babyface.'

The phrase was passed down the line until it finally reached a small boy with a haircut that was so short and crude it looked like he'd been run over by a lawnmower. He also passed on the request. 'Get Babyface . . . What am I talking about? I am Babyface.'

Bugsy passed a baseball bat down the human chain until it eventually ended up in the hands of the diminutive figure. Babyface talked himself into levels of bravery he wasn't sure he had, mumbling like a boxer before a fight. 'Right. Thanks. That's just what I need. O.K., now I've got to get out there. I've got to have courage. Big courage.'

At the top of the queue. Bugsy waited impatiently.

'What's the matter with him, Leroy?'

'I don't know, Bugsy. Babyface, will you get out there.'

'I'm scared,' came back tiny Babyface's reply. 'There's too many of them for me.'

Leroy's voice was gruff and direct. 'Babyface, get out there.'

Babyface did up the one remaining button on his shabby jacket and put his hat on straight, muttering, 'O.K., O.K. Right. I've gotta have courage now. I'm gonna be famous.'

With that, he crawled away from the others, and, picking his way through the barrels as silently as his hobnail boots would allow him, he sneaked up to Dock 17 and the unsuspecting hoods. Very carefully, he edged closer. Four of the hoods were in the middle of a game of poker and wouldn't have seen him if he'd ridden up on a tricycle. But two others were scouring the walls and the dockland alleyways almost as if they were expecting trouble. Babyface had crept to within ten feet of the hoods and was about to make his move—which was just as well, because the hood on the roof spotted him.

Babyface dashed out of hiding, and, with a loud shriek of 'Geronimo!', rushed straight at the card-playing guards and cracked one of them over the head. Even before the guard had slumped across the table, knocking cards and chips to the ground, Babyface was running as fast as his little legs could take him in the direction of Bugsy, Leroy and the down-and-outs. The baseball guards gathered their wits together and raced after him. Babyface reached the olive oil warehouse scarcely ten yards in front of them. He dashed into one of the doors and yelled a loud, if not terribly subtle, invitation.

'You bunch of dummies!'

The guards rose to the bait. One after another they piled into the warehouse. This was a big mistake for the Dandy Dan watchdogs. No sooner had the last baseball hood run inside, than the hidden down-and-outs jumped out from their refuge behind the barrels and slammed the door shut, securing it with a thick metal chain and an enormous padlock that wouldn't have looked out of place in Alcatraz prison. Babyface, meanwhile, had managed to squeeze himself out through a narrow ventilation shaft that no one wider or bigger than him could even attempt. Fortunately, most people in New York were wider and bigger than Babyface, and the baseball guards were no exception. They pummelled on the wooden doors and yelled and screamed abuse, but to no avail. The chain held firm and the down-and-outs let out a triumphant roar as they made their way across the wharf to the Splurge Inc. warehouse—and the stairway to the guns.

29. WE KNOW YOU'RE IN THERE

The two swing doors nearly broke from their hinges as the enthusiastic crowd of boys burst through. They were no longer wearing masks of misery. They were brighter, happier, and their eyes sparkled. There were smiles on faces that had long forgotten how nice it was to smile.

Bugsy directed his newly found army towards the piles of long wooden boxes, along the sides of which were stencilled in black letters the words, *The Splurge Imports Company Inc. Dock 17, East River'*. Leroy took a large metal crowbar and began levering off the lids of the boxes. Grubby hands clawed at the protective packing straw to reveal the splurge guns.

Bugsy and Babyface handed out sacks, the guns were quickly loaded into them, and soon the floor was a mess of straw and empty boxes. Absentmindedly, Leroy picked up some straw from the floor and put it on his head. The other down-and-outs laughed as he wriggled and giggled in his makeshift blonde wig. Bugsy, however, was not amused.

'Leroy, what do you think you're doing? Knock it off, will you? This is serious.'

Leroy stepped off the box on which he was performing.

'Sorry, Bugsy.'

'Right. Hurry it along now. There's no time to fool around.'

Bugsy was right. There was no time to fool around. Even less time than he thought, in fact, because at that moment Captain Smolsky and Lieutenant O'Dreary arrived, with two carloads of uniformed police.

The policemen's driving was about as good as their detective work, and the rear car smashed into the front sedan with a loud crunch. However, as it was by no means the first time this had happened, Smolsky jumped out of the front vehicle without even commenting on the collision. The rest of his men huddled around him for protection. O'Dreary handed him a loudhailer and the confident police

119

captain put it to his mouth to speak. What, in fact, came out of the other end of the funnel was a cross between an aggressive Bronx shout and a dubious Polish squeak.

'O.K., you guys. We know you're in there.'

Smolsky had never been the most original of policemen, and he had seen too many movies to fluff his lines now. 'I'll give you ten seconds to give yourselves up. It's no use. You're surrounded. Come out with your hands up.'

There was complete silence from the warehouse. O'Dreary checked his notebook to see if they'd come to the right place. Smolsky continued his impersonation of a tough cop. 'Smart guys, huh? O.K. I'll count to ten and then we're coming in to get you.'

The rest of the cops took out their truncheons and held them ceremoniously at the ready. Each one darted a quick look at Smolsky. They wanted to say they were ready to follow him to the ends of the earth if necessary. It was a confident offer, as Smolsky would be bound to get lost long before then.

Inside the warehouse, the original enthusiastic hubbub had turned to complete silence. Anxiety was written on the faces of all the down-and-outs as they looked at the blank end wall. If someone had dropped a pin at that moment it would have sounded like a Ford T starting handle.

Babyface gulped loudly. He was frightened, and his cruel haircut, fashioned by some maniacal barber, made his little face look terrified.

'What we gonna do, Bugsy?'

'I don't know, Babyface. I don't know.'

Bugsy rubbed his chin and thought. There seemed no way out. The cops had the staircase covered and there was no convenient secret hatch—or even a skylight for Leroy to try out his party trick on.

Back in the alley, Smolsky raised the metal funnel to his mouth once more. He wasn't fooling around.

'Right. I'm warning you. I'm going to start counting now. One, two, three, four, five . . . er . . . five . . .'

As the captain hesitated, on the numbers, faithful Lieutenant O'Dreary looked at him, a little concerned. He knew his boss's shortcomings. (The alphabet was another problem.) Smolsky hesitated once more.

'. . . Er . . . five . . . er, five . . .'

120

O'Dreary jumped in. 'Six, Captain. The next number's six.'

Smolsky was a little annoyed at this friendly advice. He shrugged off O'Dreary's remark in the same way as a six-year-old struggling through his first reading book. 'I know, I know . . . Six, seven, eight . . .'

In the warehouse, Bugsy and the down-and-outs looked more desperate than ever. Bugsy walked back and forth, scouring the room for possibilities. Suddenly he noticed, behind a pile of old packing cases, the tell-tale expanding door of a lift cage. That was it.

'The elevator! Quick, everybody inside.'

Leroy pulled the rusty door open and the boys piled into the old freight elevator. Bugsy tugged at the chain, conveniently and clearly marked 'Go', and the stiff machinery clanked and hummed into action as the elevator started its descent. Leroy and the down-and-outs were more than a little anxious as it shook and rattled. To say it was an old design would be an understatement. If anybody ever found out about it they'd probably want it for a museum of ancient mechanical objects. But gradually, if a little hesitantly, the elevator lowered Bugsy's gang to freedom.

Outside, Captain Smolsky carried on his impersonation of a tough New York cop. He bellowed into the loudhailer, 'Nine . . . ten . . . Right. O.K. This is it. Ready, steady, charge . . .!'

The entire force, huddled behind him, suddenly sprang into action and dashed for the warehouse door. They bumped into one another in their enthusiastic attempts to make an arrest and the front page of *Police Gazette Monthly*. Up the wooden staircase they charged, into the expected army of hoodlums. Except they were disappointed. Smolsky led his men into the warehouse to find nothing but empty boxes and straw. The only candidate for an arrest was the black and white tom cat that scooted out of a disused packing case. Smolsky whipped off his hat and dashed it across his knee with frustration.

'Rats! We missed them. Right. Where have they gone, O'Dreary?'

O'Dreary looked sharply back at Smolsky. His brow furrowed and he was momentarily stunned by having such a difficult question thrown at him.

'Well, where have they gone?' Smolsky repeated.

'Somewhere else, Captain?'

As O'Dreary squeaked out his ludicrous answer, the frustrated Smolsky belted him across the head.

'You stupid, Bronx, flat-footed . . .' Smolsky's words were drowned in the mad gurgling sounds of a desperate man. The rest of the cops made sure they kept well out of it, and cowered in the corner for safety, whilst, down below in the alley, Bugsy, Leroy, and the down-and-outs got clean away.

30. THE PAY OFF

Dandy Dan's gang lined up against their bike sedans. Bronx Charlie stroked his splurge gun, and hugged it close to him for protection. Chinese Benny Lee chewed his toothpick until it shredded at the end. His oriental grin looked even more evil than his oriental scowl. The rest of the gang looked pretty pleased with themselves as Dandy Dan walked back and forth, giving them his final address. He was dressed in a snazzy grey overcoat with a astrakhan fur collar. His tie was fastened, as ever, in an immaculate knot. He stroked his moustache with his forefinger as he spoke. He was feeling even more superior than usual.

'Gang, this is the caper that's gonna take the lid off City Hall. This is the big one.'

The faithful gang mindlessly repeated everything their dapper boss said.

'The big one.'

'The shakedown,' said Dan.

'The shakedown.'

'In fact, this is the pay off.'

'The pay off.'

'It's got to be good, it's got to be neat, and it's got to be quick.'

The gang responded with monotonous loyalty, 'It's got to be good, it's got to be neat, it's got to . . .'

However good Dandy Dan felt about the situation, the last line was enough. He bit off the end of the sentence.

'Stop repeating everything I say, will you!'

The gang's self-satisfied faces dropped a notch or two. Jackson coughed loudly to fill the embarrassed silence. Dan stroked his moustache once more and continued to be superior.

'You shouldn't have any trouble—just Fat Sam and a few dance hall girls.'

The gang laughed at Dandy Dan's joke. They always did.

'O.K. off we go, then. And good luck.'

As Dan turned to his tan sedan, his loyal hoods broke into a round of applause. Bronx Charlie stood on the running board and held his gun in the air.

'Three cheers for Dandy Dan. Hip Hip Hooray!'

Dan was overwhelmed. Not very convincingly, he waved aside their praise, and murmured, 'Too kind, boys. Too kind.'

Dan climbed into his car and Jackson slammed the door. Shoulders and Yonkers climbed into the front seat beside him, balancing their splurge guns on their knees.

'Now for Fat Sam's Grand Slam.'

At the speakeasy, Bugsy, dressed in a waiter's white jacket, organised the down-and-out gang as they changed into snazzy tuxedos to look like regular speakeasy customers. Leroy wrestled with a starched collar that sprang out as quickly as he clipped it into place. Fat Sam supervised trays of custard pies as they were brought in and tucked away secretly under the tables. The bartenders stowed their splurge guns close at hand behind the drinks counter. The dancing girls arranged their costumes as if nothing was happening. Razamataz tinkled on the piano, checking the notes. He looked nervously at the door and back to the battle preparations on the speakeasy floor.

The hubbub was deafening as Bugsy fired out instructions. Leroy checked the barrels of the guns and demonstrated how to load the splurges. Fat Sam kept close to Tallulah, Dotty and Tillie. He wanted someone to duck behind should the action get hot. Suddenly, Babyface's head appeared through the peephole that led to the bookstore. He yelled, 'They're here! They're here!'

Jelly pulled the lever and the door slid back to let Babyface in. He vaulted over Jelly and the hat-check lady as Bugsy shouted at the crowd to be ready.

'O.K., everybody. Just act like normal. Girls, off you go. Razamataz, music.'

Razamataz pounded into the piano. The dancing girls erupted into their number with a frenzy of syncopated legs and waving arms. It wasn't to last for long, however. Dan's procession of cars had arrived outside.

Dandy Dan stepped out of his sedan and stroked his moustache with his forefinger. The rest of the gang stood, splurge guns at the ready, waiting for their orders. He coughed to clear his throat and make his final speech.

'O.K., gang, I don't have to tell you how important this is to me. When you get in there, keep those fingers pumping. Because, remember, it's history you'll be writing. O.K. Let's go.'

Inside Pop Becker's bookstore, Shoulders and Benny Lee pulled the sliding door across and Dandy Dan and his gang rushed through, fingers twitching on the triggers of their guns. Dan's voice sounded more superior than ever before in his career.

'O.K., everybody. Freeze.'

The speakeasy customers turned their heads in the hoods' direction, but there were no screams. Just a silence that was broken by Sam, who popped up and shouted, 'Bugsy, guys, let them have it.'

Fat Sam's newly-found allies burst into action. The smartened up down-and-outs appeared from behind the bar, hurling custard pies and firing splurge guns. Dandy Dan's gang didn't know what had hit them.

They ducked down to avoid the barrage of missiles that whistled around their ears and occasionally hit them fair and square between the eyes. Bugsy and Leroy fired away without stopping. Soon, the entire speakeasy was a deluge of splurge, custard pies and flour bombs. In seconds, the rich dark brown walls turned to milky white as the battle raged. Pies and splurge flew in all directions. Tallulah caught one head on, and it splattered across her painted face and spread round the back of her ears. Fat Sam was a more elusive target. He ducked and dived, avoiding everything that was thrown at him. He was particularly pleased with himself when he caught Dandy Dan a direct hit on the shoulder, and then followed it up with a bulls-eye on the nose. He clapped his hands and laughed out loud—but his mouth was still open when Benny Lee returned the compliment with a crafty butterfly curver that nearly took Sam's head off. Leroy also caught one, and his smiling black face was suddenly an unsmiling white face. Fizzy tried to take refuge in the broom cupboard, but was floored by a sly one from Bronx Charlie—who, in turn, was changed into a mountain of splurge by a particularly accurate burst of shooting from Babyface. The girls in the chorus took refuge behind Razamataz's piano, but found it hard to find a safe place because the band were piled eight high in the two-foot wide space behind the instrument.

The entire speakeasy floor was covered by an eerie white cloud that made everything seem unreal. Almost everybody resembled a melting ice cream cone on a summer's day. Suddenly, Razamataz, still in his exposed position on the piano stool, ducked a vicious-looking pie from Laughing Boy, who was not coming out of the fight with as many honours as he would have liked, and fell on to the sticky, splurge-covered piano keys. The musical chord cut through the milk cloud of the splurge battle and all at once the ear-splitting din was replaced by silence. Razamataz, unaware of exactly what he'd done, did the only thing he knew how. He started singing. It was a ridiculous thing to do, considering the circumstances, but however frightened he was inside, he couldn't stop his fingers hitting the keys—the words coming out of his mouth.

Suddenly, a miracle occurred. The band picked themselves up and joined in his song, as did the chorus girls, and the barman, and the down-and-outs, and Dandy Dan's hoods. Fat Sam and Dandy Dan looked at one another in disbelief. Then Tallulah broke away from Sam and started singing too. So did Bugsy and Blousey, who had managed to escape the worst of the splurge battle. Soon the entire speakeasy was buzzing and tingling with the sound of their song and dance. Fat Sam and Dandy Dan, overcome by the ridiculous, mad, happy situation, began to join in. All rivalry was forgotten, all nastiness vanished, as people began to hug one another. Sam shook hands

with Dan. Tallulah got kissed a little too often by Leroy—
and Blousey and Bugsy sneaked for the exit, where Dandy
Dan's empty sedan stood at the kerb.

The sound of the singing seemed as loud on the open
road as it did in the speakeasy, as Bugsy and Blousey drove
off into the sunset—the kind you only see in movies, and
the kind they say dreams are made of.

> *Open your eyes and see*
> *Just what you want to see.*
> *See how nice it is to be*
> *Just what you want to be*

And that's not all!